Ernst Olcott

Margaret Worthington

Holding forth the word of life

Ernst Olcott

Margaret Worthington
Holding forth the word of life

ISBN/EAN: 9783337268855

Printed in Europe, USA, Canada, Australia, Japan

Cover: Foto ©Raphael Reischuk / pixelio.de

More available books at **www.hansebooks.com**

O honey! what's I going to do? Page 90.

THE
THOUSAND DOLLAR
PRIZE SERIES
BOSTON.
D. LOTHROP & CO.
38. & 40. CORNHILL.

MARGARET WORTHINGTON;

OR,

HOLDING FORTH THE WORD OF LIFE.

BY

KATHERINE PREVOST.

BOSTON:
PUBLISHED BY D. LOTHROP & CO.
DOVER, N. H.: G. T. DAY & CO.

Margaret Worthington.

CHAPTER I.

"Mother! Girls! I have a plan to propose."

Every one looked up eagerly as Mr. Chauncey made this remark at his breakfast-table, one October morning, for father's plans generally meant something exceedingly pleasant and profitable for all concerned in them.

"What do you say to my writing to Uncle James, and asking him to lend Margaret to us for the winter?"

"For the whole winter?"　"Cousin Mag?"　"Oh! delightful."　"You good father, to think of it."　"That's just the thing."

Such a chorus of enthusiastic answers might have been a flattering assurance to Cousin Mag of her popularity; and mamma's more quiet, but not less hearty, "I approve of your plan, decidedly," was the casting vote which alone was needed.

"Mamma, may she sit by me? I love Cousin Mag," was the next remark which made itself heard above the general family din, and which caused a laugh to extend from father himself down to the one who had provoked it. She was used to being laughed at — this little mischief-maker, Susie. The baby of the family,—a bright-eyed, curly-pated witch, — she was the pride, the pet, and the plaything of all the home-circle, and was in danger of acquiring the firm belief that big brothers and sisters were nothing more nor less than the devoted and loyal servants of Her Majesty, Sue. Nothing daunted by the reception her entreaty had met with, Sue repeated it, but was soon silenced with,

"When Cousin Mag comes it will be time enough to talk about that. We must listen, now, to what else Papa has to tell us about this nice plan of his."

"That is soon told," Papa said. "It occurred to me, only this morning, that just now, when autumn is fairly setting in, and we are all fresh from our summerings, it would be the best season of the year for Margaret to make us her long-promised visit. That started the idea; and then I thought, why not try to persuade James and Helen to let us have her for the whole winter? She knows very little, practically, of city life; and yet, I do not know of any one more thoroughly calculated to enjoy a more extensive acquaintance with cultivated people than she can have off there, among the mountains. Of course, living in a college town, she has always been thrown with literary people; but still, excepting for a few weeks in the summer, the circle is narrow, and life is a sort of treadmill with them. It will do her good to live in the midst of a bustle for a while, and she will revel in the art galleries, and the concert halls, to say nothing of the opera, which promises to be very fine this winter, and all the rest of the gayeties."

"Oh! and besides, Papa, she can take lessons with us; and I know she has been longing to study German, and has had no opportunity. Uncle James did speak of asking Professor Nollet to give her lessons, but he said it really went against his conscience to ask him to tax his voice one bit more, his throat is so weak now."

"Of course, if she comes, she will be one with you in any of the occupations she would enjoy."

"But, Mamma," said Kitty, "do you really think they will let her come for the whole winter. How will they ever get along without her? Dear me! we think we are lost if one of us goes away for a month; and here we are, six of us, while they have only three. And I know those boys think Mag is nothing short of perfection. Mag must help them with their lessons; Mag must look at their chemical attempts; Mag must mend their gloves; Mag must do this, and Mag must do that. She seems to enjoy it all as well as they do, and there are not half enough pet names in the English language. They invent a dozen or two a day for her."

"She is a good, unselfish creature," her

mother replied; "and I am very sure she
will bring nothing but pleasure among us if
she does come; so the best way is for Papa
to write at once, and let this mighty matter
be discussed at Rowenah. For my own
part, I imagine that she will come. Of
course, I don't know, but I think her father
will rejoice at the greater advantages for
lessons and all that she will find here."

"Well, then, I'll write to-day. So you
impatient youngsters need not have this terrible suspense to endure very long. But it is
time I was on my way down town. Don't
agonize, Kit. What an excitable creature you
are! one would think it was a matter of life
or death to you."

"Well, Papa, I can't help it. I do think
it will be nearly bliss to be in the same
house with Mag for weeks and months together. May I just write a wee note to

her myself, too, and tell her she will break my heart if she disappoints us? "

" You may write as much as you please, Childie — why not? I only hope, when the great matters of life come, you will meet them with a little more ballast. Well, good morning, — I'm off."

CHAPTER II.

———

" You dear old Madgie," so Kit's harum-
scarum note began, " I'm in a perfect flut-
ter, and have been ever since Papa broached
a subject at the breakfast-table this morning, concerning which his letter will en-
lighten you. I have got permission to add
my scrawl, just to say, Do, please, come.
If you don't, why you will break my heart,
that's all. Just think what a calamity that
would be. If you could have been at the
table and heard the enthusiasm the mere
mention of your name aroused, you couldn't,

no, you couldn't, refuse. Laura is just as anxious to see you as I am, only she is so different. I sigh for her calm repose, her powers of self-control, but so far, alas! I have sighed in vain. But never mind all this now; only come, that's the main point, at present, and we will discuss the others bye and bye.

Your own expectant Kit."

"There, Laura, if that don't persuade her, my power amounts to nothing. What are you about, I should like to know! Drawing as calmly as if nothing had happened. Why, I could no more hold a pencil steadily than I could fly, Laura; nor half so easily, I.think. Just imagine having that duck of a Mag here the whole winter. Laura! do answer me. I declare, you provoke me! I could almost think — it can't be — surely it can't be, that there is anything disagreeable to you in the idea. I am sure you have always loved Mag just as we all have."

"Well, Kitty, I am a little ashamed of myself, and I don't think I should confess my feelings to any one else; but to tell the truth, I am a little afraid to have Mag come here.''

'' Afraid of Mag Worthington ! '' Kitty laughed her joyous, merry laugh, which was so charming and so contagious. '' Afraid of Mag ! Well, that is the wildest, most unaccountable, of all your vagaries. I cannot imagine anything more unlikely. You may as well lay aside your pencil at once, for I assure you I shall not budge till you tell me what you mean."

'' Well, my dear, if you can be quiet long enough to give me a chance, I will try to . tell you, though I am not sure that I understand my own feelings well enough to put them into words. But don't you know, last spring we heard that Mag had joined the church? Now, as you say, I have always loved Mag dearly, but then, we have not seen her since that time, and how do we know what change that may have produced?"

"Joined the church! so she has. How strange that I should have forgotten it. I guess it went in one ear and out of the other, as most such things do with me."

Kitty looked a little disconcerted for a few minutes, and her countenance fell. Still, as it was not her way to be long cast down about anything, and as she had, pre-eminently, the faculty of looking at the bright side of everything, she regained her flow of spirits in a few moments.

"After all, Laura, I don't see what difference that can make. Joining the church can't take away one's love for pictures, can it, or one's desire to study? And I'm sure it cannot have spoiled Mag's glorious alto voice."

" No, it can't do any of these. But can it not make one very gloomy and stupid? Suppose Mag thinks her voice can only be used for hymns, then what shall we do when Fred calls for one of our old quartettes? And, Kit, don't you remember that meddling, fanatical, some sort of a girl at school, Louise Somers? I am sure she thought it was a sin to laugh; and, as to believing in liberty of conscience, she might as well have been Philip II., or even Alva himself, excepting that she was born in a free country, and could not send us all to the stake. If we did not think just as she did, we were utterly lost; and I never shall forget the sanctimonious roll of her eyes at any harmless joke. She was a member of the church. What if Mag should be like that? "

"Oh! but Laura, you know that is impossible. Mag could never be underhanded
or a prig, and I am sure Louise Somers was
both. Besides, Mag is a lady, born and
bred; and even if we disagreed about principles and such matters, she would not force
her own opinions upon us. I don't even
believe she would have that Pharisaical way
about her. There were other girls at school
who were members of the church, too, and
I don't believe every one must be like the
most disagreeable specimen of womanhood I
ever met. Look at dear old Poll! I am
sure there never was a merrier romp than
she was when we kept within proper
bounds, though she was the first to with-
draw when any questionable prank was suggested. Louise Somers, indeed! No; Mag
Worthington and she are as far apart as the
two poles of a magnet, and I don't believe

any principle of religion, or natural philosophy, either, would draw them together."

" Well, dear, perhaps I am foolish — I hope I am mistaken. As you say, there were other girls at school besides Louise Somers, who were church members, and I did respect some of them.   The real earnest ones, who did their own duty, and did not feel called upon to be always preaching, would have influenced me much sooner than the interfering ones; in fact, I was more than once put to the blush by their quiet example, when sermonizing would have only made me mad. I always wanted to say to Louise, ' Practice what you preach, ma'mselle.'   Indeed, I believe I did say so once, though I was sorry for it afterwards, because she may have been in earnest, after all. However, we have wandered far away from Mag, and if her religion has not spoiled her, I am very sure you will not enjoy her any more than I shall, though you will rave more, and show it more."

Laura's doubts were the only ones expressed or felt respecting the delight Margaret's visit would give, if she should accept Mr. Chauncey's invitation. She was the favorite cousin of the whole family, nor was her popularity undeserved. The only daughter of a professor in one of our New England colleges, she had been most carefully educated, for, although her father was not entirely dependent upon his salary, his means were not large enough to admit the expectation of his being able to leave his family provided with an ample inheritance, and the possibility of a teacher's life had been constantly before Margaret's eyes from early girlhood. So far, there had been no call for the exercise of her talent in that direction, and though she would never have been one to shrink from any path of duty, she was very thankful to be able to consider home her true sphere. In their quiet village she had developed from a thoughtful, attractive child into an intelligent, cultivated, even accomplished, girl; and at the age of twenty, when our story opens, she was the pride and companion of her father, the tender and warm-hearted confidant of her mother, and, as Kitty had stated it, "nothing short of perfection" in the eyes of Walter and Rob, her younger brothers. Nor had her mind been cultivated at the expense of her heart, for " from a child " she had " known the Scriptures, and had been thoroughly instructed in the principles of the doctrines of Christ." Of a peculiarly sensitive, conscientious disposition, she had long seemed to her parents like one who had passed from death unto life, and she had many times felt that Jesus was indeed her Saviour, yet she had shrunk from publicly professing her faith in Him, until the spring of the year in which we have made her acquaintance. Then had she seemed to obtain a "full assurance of faith." She knew whom she had believed, and hesitated not to confess Him before men; and after once deciding to take this step, she seemed entirely to lose the shrinking she had felt before, and to be more than willing to be the avowed disciple of the Lord.

Her cousins fancied that some strange transformation must have been caused by this profession. To them, as yet, the service of Christ meant thraldom, not "the glorious liberty" of the children of God. They pictured her as saddened, or at least sobered, by the presence of Him whom she knew to

be the chief source of all her joy and happiness; they thought she must be bowed
down beneath the whole armor of God,
little understanding that " His yoke is easy
and his burden light."

CHAPTER III.

A letter from Uncle Henry, the best beloved brother of her mother, was always a treat to Margaret; but he was a good correspondent, and very fond of his niece, so that she was not at all surprised when Rob, the family mail-carrier, bounded into the library, where all the family had assembled, and from among a pile of papers and letters for his father, produced one for Mag. News from the family of city cousins was always shared by all, but still Mag glanced over her letter quietly, at first. She was a good deal excited before she finished it, and a conflicting tumult of reasons for accepting, and reasons for declining, her uncle's invitation, had suggested themselves simultaneously, while charming visions of a city life, and depressing anticipations of homesickness, made her brain reel. She passed the letter to her mother, saying, " Read it aloud, Mamma. I am sure Uncle Henry is the best uncle living ;" and Professor Worthington laid aside his own letters, while Walter and Rob settled into quietness, as Mrs. Worthington read :

" My dear Margaret :

Here we are, all at home again in New York, thoroughly recruited by our summer travels, and ready for any amount of winter work. The girls have already started with some of their lessons, and I hear great plans of German, to be begun in a week or two. New York is at its best, just now; every one so fresh and so glad to be at home, and not sorry, either, to settle down to regular employments after a long vacation. We held a family caucus at our breakfast-table, this morning, and it was then and there unanimously decided that our circle was incomplete; that one more must be added to ensure our thorough enjoyment of the winter, and that that one was yourself. When, a year ago, you made us your last flying visit, it did not half satisfy us. I write to-day, therefore, to urge you to make up your mind to spend the whole of this winter with us. Kitty is writing this morning, also, and I do not doubt her powers of persuasion are greater than mine, but perhaps my words may have the most weight, after all. I know the opportunities of improvement will tempt you more than anything else, so I will begin with those arguments, and assure you that you shall study to your heart's utmost content. The girls mean to accomplish a great deal this winter, and of course you would make one at any of their lessons which attract you. As to other matters, we have many pleasant people among us whom you will enjoy, and who would be glad to know your father's daughter, even were she different from what we know her to be. Then Parepa and Ole Bull are both to visit us, to say nothing of a fine oratorio series, and the prospect of a good opera. Two or three famous actors have been secured, and though lectures have not yet been announced, you know we generally have as many of those as we can manage to digest. We flatter ourselves the programme will attract you; and your aunt and I, to say nothing of your cousins, feel that it will give us much pleasure to have you with us. Of course the decision rests with your father and mother, but you must give them both our love, and tell them we will take the best care of you. Perhaps we will try to recompense them, in a measure, by letting them see more of Frank than they have hitherto done, for while Fred is not only satisfied with, but enthusiastic over, his choice of a business life, Frank's ambition is only bounded by a seat on the bench, and he must enter college in a year. I do not say certainly that he will try old Spearmouth, but I have too much love for my Alma Mater to pass it by without consideration. Do not decide too hurriedly, if there is any danger of your disappointing us, but believe that the sooner you come, and the longer you stay, the better you will please

Your loving uncle,
HENRY CHAUNCEY.

"Well, Maggie, what do you say?"

"O Mother, I don't know what to say! I

should enjoy it, of course, ever so much, and it is wonderfully kind of Uncle Henry to propose it; but I hate the thought of leaving home."

" Leaving home for the winter! Well, I will settle that for you," Bob burst forth. " It is not to be thought of for a moment. I should like to know what we would do without you. A pretty plan, indeed. Just ask Uncle Henry how he would like to give up Kitty; and, if he should, he would still have Laura. Why, imagine home without you! "

" Yes, indeed,'' said more thoughtful mother. " If you want to make a little visit in New York, do go, and tell Uncle Henry he is very kind; but we want you ourselves, and the idea of doing without you is preposterous."

" Well, boys, I don't know. It would

be grand to study so much; and, Father, what do you think? ”

“ That we should all miss you sadly, my daughter; but, that I am by no means sure that the invitation should be declined. It is certainly most thoughtful in Uncle Henry, and it would do you a world of good. Rowenah is but a wee bit of the world, and your horizon is very circumscribed. It will be pleasant, and very profitable, to be at Uncle Henry’s; his friends are of the very first class. I do not mean only of the wealthiest, but of the best educated, best informed, most highly cultivated. Your former visits there, — indeed, you have made but one since you left school, — have been such short ones that you have been occupied with sight-seeing too steadily to have more than a bird’s-eye view of anything; and, altogether, — ”

“ Altogether,” Mrs. Worthington interrupted her husband, " altogether, it seems to me that Uncle Henry's suggestion comes from beyond him. It is a thing to be accepted, and to be most thankful for, — thankful, I mean, to Him ' Who giveth us all things richly to enjoy.' You know how you have longed to study German, and to go on with music, and now you can do both. And then, if you ever should need to teach, you will have just so many more resources, and if not, — why, God never gives us talents or acquisitions without giving us occasions for using them. So it strikes me, but still the decision must rest with yourself. We do not, any of us, want to spare you, excepting as it is for your own good.' '

" Well, Mamma," both the boys began, but Rob, as usual, got the ascendency. " I never thought you would take Uncle Henry's side ! Margery, darling, please don't go.

Would you go, and spoil a fellow's comfort
for the whole winter? "

" Rather uncomplimentary to the rest of
us, Rob," said his father.

" O well, Papa, you know I don't mean
that, — of course you know what I mean.
I just mean that none of us can spare each
other.   And Mag is so, — so, — bully ! "

" But, really and truly, Madge, do you
want to go?'' put in Walter.   " That seems
to be the main point."

" It's hard to say, Walt.   I want to, and
I don't want to.   Uncle Henry's house is
the next thing to home, you know, and the
girls are the dearest cousins that ever were;
and the German, and the music, and the
art-galleries, and the studios, are all great
temptations.   But, then, on the other
hand, — ''

" Be it ever so humble, there's no place
like home,'' sang Rob in a serio-comic air,

as he put his hands into his pockets and
walked out of the room. Into his own sanctum he went, and there to give vent to his
feelings. He let forth a torrent of invective
against Uncle Henry for presuming to think
of having Mag; against Papa and Mamma
for taking the matter into consideration; and
finally, against himself, somewhat in this
wise :

" What a selfish old pig I am, any way.
I suppose Margery would enjoy it, and it
would be too bad for her to miss the
chance. I don't believe it was altogether
the idea of losing her that made me so fu-
rious, after all. But it does make me so
mad to hear mother and Mag talk about
teaching. What's the use of a girl having
two brothers, I should like to know, if we
can't support her? However, if she wants
to learn, let her. I'll go back and see what
decision they've come to, any way."

They had not come to any. Kitty's note had been read and discussed, but Mr. Worthington had said:

" This is Saturday ; so you need not write to your Uncle till Monday morning, my dear. We will all think quietly about it over Sabbath, and that will give us plenty of time."

So they had separated to their several duties ; but in two minds, at least, there was not much quiet. Mrs. Worthington had all the unselfishness common to mothers, and not for worlds would she have urged her daughter to any course which seemed opposed to her enjoyment and improvement ; yet her heart could not but shrink from the idea of parting with her who was daily growing less the child and more the friend. Who, as she grew womanly, grew also more companionable. From whom there were no

longer any secrets. Nay, of whom counsel
was even sometimes sought.

To Margaret it seemed that the more she
thought of the matter, the more it became
impossible to decide. Not only did there
seem to be conflicting pleasures, but duties.
Would it be right to go? Was she not
needed at home? She, the only daughter,
could she, ought she, to be spared? The
boys would miss her, and, would they not
need her? And while they and her father
were in college,—they as students, he busy
with his classes,—would not her mother be
alone a good deal? And her Sabbath class!
There were too few teachers, already. Was
it right for one more voluntarily to desert?
Moreover, who would look after poor Aunt
Dinah, the old colored woman, too deaf to
hear in church, untaught in letters, yet with
ears open for the word of life, — yea, with
a heart full of the wisdom which maketh

wise unto salvation? Margaret had, almost ever since she had learned to read, spent an hour with Aunt Dinah on the Sabbath, and visited her often during the week. And though it was a great strain to make the voice penetrate those closed ears, she seldom passed more enjoyable hours, for Aunt Dinah had spent long years in the service of the Master. And, as in simple words, at which the wise of this world might have jeered, she told her rich experience, Margaret had almost envied her tribulations which had worked such patience, since patience had brought experience, and experience, hope. Aunt Dinah was very old now. Perhaps before a whole winter had passed she would have entered into the inheritance for which she yearned. And, since not only the aged pass away, Margaret could not repress a thrill of fear as the thought crossed her mind, what breaks might not be made

in the circle of home friends in the course
of a few months! Yet, on the other hand,
would it be treating Uncle Henry's invitation with the warm reception it deserved,
to decline it altogether? Her mother's
words, " It comes from beyond him," helped
her most of all; and when she had committed
it to God, her mind was more calm, and she
felt that they would all be guided in this
matter by Him who never yet has failed His
people.

At tea, and throughout the evening, little
but this was spoken of, and pros and cons
were repeated over and over again. But Mr.
and Mrs. Worthington grew more and more
in favor of the plan. And Margaret herself, with the natural desire of young people
for change, could not but dwell on the
tempting prospects held out to her in the
letter.

On Sunday, as she sat in church, she

seemed like one in a dream. What the
sermon was she hardly knew, excepting that
every word seemed to take some reference
to her projected visit, though it had not
been spoken of outside of the home circle.
The word that she carried home with her
was Moses' prayer: "If thy presence go
not with us, carry us not up hence." And
on that she stayed herself.

It may seem to many that a simple visit
to an uncle's house is not a matter of such
great importance. But Margaret had not
often been away from home, excepting with
her parents. Moreover, she was in the
habit of weighing even smaller matters than
this with a great deal of care; for both con-
scientiousness and timidity were prominent
traits in her character. She was not very
impulsive, and could not decide a question
till both sides had been carefully weighed;
but when she had once decided that a thing

was right, she was unyielding, and no attractions on the other side caused her to cast a look of regret towards them.

At length, on Sunday evening, the matter was finally talked over, and Margaret said:

"Well, Mother, I have but one ground of hesitation left, and that is your loneliness."

"Then do not hesitate any longer, my child, but accept your uncle's invitation at once. It is not as if I were in ill-health, or over-taxed in any way. And if any contingency should arise to make your presence necessary, New York is not so very far off."

"I'll go and have the measles, or do something desperate, see if I don't," growled Rob.

"As you had them some years ago, you will have to find some other plan," answered his mother, laughing. "Don't you think Mother can fill Mag's place?"

"O yes, ma'am! especially in coasting." And the home boy, forgetting the Freshman dignity so lately assumed, threw his arms around his mother's waist with a loving clasp.

"Well, Marge, if you are going away, let us have as much music as possible in the mean time," said Walter, opening the piano. "What shall we begin with, Mamma,—your favorite, ' Silently the shades of evening? '"

That, and many another dear old hymn, was sung by voices which appreciated the melodies; from hearts full of the meaning of the words, and then they separated for the night.

In her room, Margaret looked her visit to New York in the face, seeing many new aspects at every gaze. "How it will increase my responsibilities!" was her last thought that night. "Here, at home, and in this quiet place, it seems so easy to be a Christian, with every one expecting it of me, and helping me on my way. But in the city, at Uncle Henry's, and with those gay girls, shall I not meet with temptations that I never dreamed of? ‘ Deliver me from evil,’ ” she prayed. And swift as an angel messenger came the assurance, “ God is faithful, who will not suffer you to be tempted above that ye are able, but will, with the temptation, also make a way of escape, that ye may be able to bear it.” And Margaret's sleep that night was not broken by any apprehension of temptation greater than she could bear.

CHAPTER IV.

On Monday, as soon as Margaret had written her letter to her uncle and deposited it in the office, she hastened to communicate her expected departure to her intimate friend, Emily Robertson, the daughter of the village pastor. The two girls had been playmates from their earliest childhood; had shared with each other the thousand confidences of girlhood, and had finally set the seal to their friendship on that solemnly happy day when they had taken their seats together at the Master's table. Since then, their lives had been almost as one, although, as so often happens, their characters and dispositions were almost the reverse of each other, the one seeming to supply what the other lacked. Margaret had not spoken even to Emily of her invitation, till the acceptance had been written. Why, she hardly knew, for there had been no reason for concealing it; but it was rather her habit to be quiet about a thing while it was yet undecided. It was a trait for which Emily scolded her. As she said, Margaret always knew even her half-formed purpose, while she only knew Margaret's when she was ready for action. But the habit still remained. Now, however, she was eager to communicate the news to her friend, that they might discuss it in all its phases. So she hastened to the parsonage, and challenged Emily to a walk.

"It's a glorious morning, real October;

and, besides, I have a piece of news for you."

So off they started, over the fallen leaves which early frosts had dislodged from their summer homes, under the red maple and the yellow elm, across the fields and by the river-side, drinking in the bracing air, and revelling in the mellow autumn sunlight.

"Now for your news, Mag!" was Emily's first exclamation, as they started from the house.

"Well, dear, perhaps you will not be so eager when you hear what it is. I've just mailed a letter, promising to spend the whole winter in New York."

"At your Uncle Henry's? O, how glad I am! what a glorious time you will have!" was the glowing, unselfish response. "But what a heartless creature you are, to be willing to leave us all, me in particular, of course I mean, just when we had made all our winter plans for reading and studying together, and stored them away in our brains like apples in the cellar, to be brought out and enjoyed around the fireside at fit seasons."

" I know it, Em ; and, indeed, it took me a long time to decide. I do hate to go away from home for a whole season. And, I got Uncle Henry's letter inviting me, on Saturday. At first, I could not tell what would be the right thing to do. Being the only daughter, I know Mother will be lonely, and that the boys will miss me, to say nothing of my Sunday class, and Aunt Dinah, — "

" And Em Robertson, — "

" O well, you will miss me, of course ; but you do not need me, and the arguments on the other side are very weighty. Think of the lessons I shall take. Music and singing and German. And the girls are always reading French, and I shall try to make them speak it; for, having been abroad, of course they are much more familiar with its colloquial phrases than I am; and then Father is delighted that I should have the opportunity of meeting more people, his old friends, too, so that, altogether, this side seemed to more than counterbalance the other, and go I shall.''

"Of course you will. I think you would be very foolish to do otherwise; and, indeed, I am glad you are going. It is just what will suit you, and do you good. I don't believe I should hesitate a moment if such a chance were offered me; but, unfortunately, our relatives are all country people like ourselves."

"Yes, I don't doubt you would have settled it all in a minute, and sent off an answer by the evening mail. O Em, it's a pity you could not give me a little of your decision! I cannot help seeing two sides to every question.”

“ My dear Mag! If I had your prudence and forethought, I think I should be too happy. I rush pell-mell into things, and after I have gone into some wild scheme, I find myself in the midst of a swamp, and wonder how I shall ever get out of it or through it.”

“ But as you always contrive to do one thing or the other very successfully, I don’t see but that your way is as good as any other. Still, that is neither here nor there. As to my visit, — ”

“ Yes, your visit. Please, marm, don’t go and get so stuck-up with them fine city folks that you won’t recognize your old friends.” And the comical girl dropped a funny little courtesy to her friend.

“ Em! How can you? I don’t think you

need fear my constancy. But now I want to talk about some things I have been thinking, but that I have not said to any one. You don't know Laura and Kitty. You were away when they were here."

" Yes, and I always regretted it so much, for I know I should like them, and I like to know my friend's friends, any way."

" Well, you know all about them. What fine girls they are, real good hearted, splendidly educated, of fascinating manners, and not one bit spoiled by all their money or their trip to Europe. Laura, you know, is older, and Kit is younger, than I; but now the difference is not as observable as when we were children. And we are all perfectly companionable, and yet, do you know, I dread being with them for so long? "

" Dread it! What can you mean, Margie? I should think it would be every way delightful."

" And so it would, Em, but for one thing ; and, perhaps it is cowardice in me to shrink from that. Think of the influence I ought to exert. They are not Christians, you know."

" Are they not? O, I am sorry for that ! But your uncle and aunt are? "

" No, dear ; at least, not professedly so. As far as I know, I shall be alone there. And I cannot help dreading that."

" But, Margie, perhaps that is the very reason for your visit, — to strengthen you, and to give you work to do. Who knows but that you may lead both the girls to think it worth while to be Christians? "

" O Emmie, if I only could ! I have thought about it so much these last two days ; but the more I think the more impossible it seems. For, from Uncle Henry down, they are outwardly such a faultless family, so much better than many who call themselves Christians, that they must be the hardest to reach. I have heard Mother compare Uncle Henry, — you know she idolizes him, — to the young ruler whom even Jesus loved; and they are all the same. I know when I was there last it often seemed as if they must be governed by love to God, their intercourse with each other was so delightful. And yet, there was no recognition of Him that I could discover.''

'' They go to church, do they not? ''

'' O yes, indeed! Always in the morning, and are the staunchest Presbyterians, boys and all. And Uncle Henry is always depended upon for large contributions to all their missionary and benevolent enterprises. He is very liberal, and he believes in the spread of the gospel as a moralizing and civilizing agent. At least, — oh! he goes farther than that. He respects religion, when it is honest and genuine; but he has no patience with cant or hypocrisy. And he has seen so many church members whom he charges with inconsistency, that he has grown almost to suspect a man of all sorts of deceit, just because he professes to be a Christian."

"But, Mag, there must be some Christians among his friends who are earnest and sincere."

"Of course there are; a great many. But none of them are perfect, you know. And don't you know the thoroughly moral, upright man is always the most exacting in his requirements of Christians? He sees some, perhaps, who do things that he would scorn to do, and he does not see the heart-achings and the repentance that follow the transgression. Nay, more than that; he does not, perhaps, even appreciate the force of the temptation, for he has never been tempted in the same manner. So he condemns his fellow-sinner for what he sees amiss in him; and, because his brother is not perfect, will not yield his own proud heart to the Saviour. Aunt Alice is very lovely, but I do not know her as well as I do Uncle Henry. I have never had a letter from her, and she does not write very often to Mother. She is a languid beauty, and Uncle Henry has always spared her every exertion, even that of letter-writing. Her own family idolize her, and the slightest expression of a wish from her lips is more to them than a positive command from some parents. Laura is very dignified, and sometimes, I believe, very haughty. I should suppose she would be the last person in the world to bear any reminder of duty, or even any appeal. Still, she is a noble creature, who inspires me with a great deal of enthusiasm whenever I am with her. I think she is very like Uncle Henry, and of course that would be enough for me.”

“ And Kitty?”

“ Kitty is very impulsive, and very, very affectionate. She sent me a most characteristic note with Uncle Henry’s invitation. Here it is; read it, if you want to.”

“ I should like Kitty, I know,” was Emily’s comment. “ But Laura attracts me especially. Margaret, it seems to me that God is sending you there to let your light shine.”

“ But what if it should only flicker, Em? ”

“ If God sends you there, dear, I am sure it will not be without grace to glorify Him. Tell me about the rest of your Uncle’s family.”

“ Well, Fred is just about my age, — between Laura and Kitty. He is in business with Uncle Henry. Frank expects to enter college next fall, and may come here. I do not know the boys very well, but they are fine fellows, I believe, and have always been very kind to me when we have been together. Then there are two little ones, Arthur, about eleven years old, and little Susie. She was a beauty, as a baby, and we were great friends when I was there. The girls write that she has not forgotten my visit, yet."

"Well, Margie, I do not see but that you will have everything to make you have a happy winter."

"Except that I shall not be at home."

"Oh! but you will not be home-sick if everything goes on well. Your mother will not suffer from your absence, and I suppose you could come home at any time, if any necessity should arise?"

"Of course I can. And Cousin Charlotte had promised Mother, before this matter was broached, that she would make her a long visit this winter, so that will break the interval. Yes, I expect I shall have a real good time, but I have not told you everything that worries me, yet."

"What else, then?"

"Why, you know Uncle Henry speaks of the opera; and that brought up to my mind all the difficult questions about amusements. It has been very easy, so far, away from the noise of the city, and with no greater excitement than a fair, or a second-rate concert, to decry all the questionable amusements as sinful; but I have never felt at all clear about them. I have always been content to leave the matter, because it has not been a personal thing; but now, the time has come when I must decide concerning each one. And, if I decide against them, I must be well furnished with arguments, to prove that my position is the right one. No mere ' Because ' will satisfy Uncle Henry or the girls."

" What do your father and mother think of them ? "

" Mother has never been to an opera, and never would go ; and Father gave it up long ago. Yet, I do not think that either of them would unhesitatingly pronounce it an unpardonable sin to go occasonally, or that they would forbid our going. I do not know ; as I have said, I never had any rea- son for thinking particularly about these matters, and so I have only formed hasty and incomplete views of them."

" I am sure I cannot advise you about it, Mag. Being a minister's daughter, I have always felt that I did not need any partic- ular opinions on the subject."

" But, Em, I don't believe in that doc- trine, at all. I am sure that what is wrong for you, is wrong for me, especially a matter embracing such wide generalities. And if I were satisfied that it were right for me to go to the opera, I should be perfectly willing to have my minister meet me there. For although, of course, his influence is more extensive than mine, is not mine as great, as far as it goes? God gave some apostles, and some teachers; but He only gave one way of salvation, one rule of life."

"That is a new idea to me; but it sounds as if you were right. I don't know, I am sure. Religion was never meant to debar us from all recreation. But a true line must be drawn somewhere between Christ's servants and those who are not. And where shall it be? It seems to me that your father and mother will tell you what they wish and expect."

"Perhaps they will; and, if they do, of course the matter of going or not going will be settled. At the same time, even then, I should want to know the arguments on both sides; and you see I don't. It is not only the theatre and the opera,— it is cards and billiards (they have a billiard room,) and all the rest."

" As to dancing, it seems to me, without knowing a very great deal about it, that the square dances, taken in moderation, cannot be productive of any harm, though I know people do condemn all dancing, without any reservation. I really don't know what to say, Mag."

" Well, Em, I wish you would think these matters over and help me. Of course you will write very often, and I shall write you all my difficulties. I feel better, already, for having talked with you. It seems to take off half a burden, to share it."

" About Aunt Dinah, Mag. Do you think she would let me read to her sometimes?"

"O, Em! Will you, really, you dear girl? I am sure that is being a friend in need."

"I cannot promise to be as regular as you have been, Mag, because I have more to occupy me at home; but I should love to take your place in a measure, and she must not be left alone."

"O, thank you, Emily, so much! That takes a great deal off my mind. I really have been afraid to think of telling her I was going; for she is lost unless some one reads to her. But you will be a splendid substitute, and I can promise you will not be sorry to have undertaken it."

"I know I shall not. I have always half envied you your intercourse with her. But you began to visit her before I had any missionary zeal at all; and now she thinks no one quite like you."

"Dear old Aunt Dinah! I bless her often

for the good she has done me. Her prayers,
alone, more than repay one for anything they
do for her. And when she gets accustomed
to your voice you will find that she can
follow the reading pretty well, and her remarks are often better than a sermon."

"How soon shall you go?"

"I do not know. In about a fortnight,
I suppose; possibly sooner, for as I am to
study with the girls, and as they have begun some lessons already, the sooner I get
there the less I shall have to make up."

"What are they studying?"

"I hardly know. Principally the languages, I presume, for they have both finished school."

"Well, my dear, if you never have any
other teaching to do, you may communicate
all your knowledge of German to me, for I
don't see any other possibility of learning
it."

So ended both walk and talk, as the girls reached Mr. Worthington's gate, and Margaret went in with a very much lighter heart and more composed mind than she had when she went out.

CHAPTER V.

———

" Here it is, Father dear," said Kitty, as Mr. Chauncey entered the dining room on Tuesday morning. " I have been looking at the outside of it for the last fifteen minutes, and wishing the paper were transparent."

" What is it, pray? " said her father, in pretended ignorance.

" O Father ! What could it be, but Mag's letter ? Please don't tease me so. Indeed, I cannot wait another moment."

She fidgeted about the room while her

father read the letter rather deliberately, and at last she went behind his chair, and looking over his shoulder, exclaimed :

" Papa, you don't deserve to have me exercise another bit of patience; so I shall take my revenge in this way." And as her father made no objection, she read :

" My dear Uncle :

How very, very kind you are to me ! I scarcely know how to thank you for your love, as manifested always, and particularly for this invitation to spend the winter with you. At first, I thought of nothing but the delight that such a visit would give me ; but my second thoughts were not unmixed with doubts as to whether I ought to leave home for so long a time. And, I confess, it took me all yesterday to consider the matter in its various lights. Father and Mother, however, are wholly on

your side. They generally are on the side
which tends to my enjoyment; and they in-
sist upon it, that the attractions you offer
are too great to be slighted, so in a very
short time I think you may expect to see
me. I cannot tell precisely when I shall
start; for, of course, there are various little
preparations to be made, and I shall have to
find an escort, besides. But there are always
opportunities for going down in the fall, and
I shall probably be able to write definitely
in a few days. Please give my best love
to all, from Aunt Alice down to Susie; and
tell Kitty that I will answer her note when
I know just when I shall go down. Good-
bye, till then.

From your most loving niece,

MARGARET WORTHINGTON.

"O, how glad I am! Are not you,
Father?" And Kitty fairly danced about

the room, exclaiming, as her mother came in — " Mag is coming, Mamma, here is her letter ! " then rushing off to meet Laura on her way down stairs, and communicate the joyful tidings to her. As they gathered around the breakfast-table little was spoken of but the letter, even Laura having dismissed, for the time being, her doubts and apprehensions, on reading its warm expressions of affection and enthusiasm. The boys, too, grew quite excited over the subject; and various plans were made for all sorts of pleasant doings when Margaret should have come.

" I wonder, Father, whether we had not better put off our German till Mag comes, and then all start together. I do not believe it will make any difference to Mr. Fluegel, for we shall, probably, go on pretty late in the spring."

" You can write a note, at all events, and

try to arrange matters with him. Perhaps you can wait, and then take four lessons a week for a while, in order to make the quarters come out the same. I should not like him to lose anything by the detention, for he needs all he can make, poor man.".

"O well, Mag is so bright she can easily catch up with us, even if we have commenced ! " said Laura. "But Mr. Fluegel is coming here to-day to arrange the hour, and we can consult him then."

"Mamma," said Susie, "where's Cousin Mag going to sleep?"'

"O Mamma ! I meant to ask you that," said Kitty. "Shall she share my room, or have the back room alone?"

"Which would you prefer? "

"O, I should like to have her with me, of course ! But I don't think that is the question. Which will she like best, I wonder ? "

" Why, I don't know. What do you think, Laura? "

" Mamma, I can hardly judge. For I like a room to myself so much that I cannot imagine any other arrangement pleasant. I should not suppose that Margaret was timid, at all; but perhaps she would rather be with Kitty."

" It seems to me, dear," said Mr. Chauncey, " that you had better give her a room alone. No matter how much people enjoy being together, there are times when perfect solitude is desirable to every one; and, therefore, I think that the better arrangement. If she has the back room, Kitty, you can run from one to the other as often as you chose; and yet you need not grow irksome to each other."

" I believe you are right, Papa,'' said Kitty. " The back room it shall be, then."

Margaret had described Mr. Chauncey's family very accurately, in her conversation with Emily, referred to in a former chapter. A less partial observer might have said that it seemed as if they must be actuated by the love of God, in their intercourse with one another. And yet it was very seldom that any earnest thought of Him crossed their minds. They went to church, to be sure, and sat under the preaching of a faithful pastor. But their attendance was a mere form; and his words, so far, had seemed to fall unheeded on their ears. He had felt, with Margaret, that their very outward faultlessness was a barrier to his approach; and knew, that they would screen themselves, as, alas! so many do, behind the inconsistencies of professing Christians. And so he had not often broached the subject to them. Do not think that he was, therefore, negligent of his duty. God was

witness to unceasing prayers and strong sup-
plications on their behalf; and often, and
sadly. He looked after them on the Sabbath, and as he met them through the week.
Often, too, did he pray for some opportunity
to speak to them, personally, when his words
would not be repelled as intrusive, or re-
sented as uncalled-for. He blended, with his
love for the Master and his zeal for the service, two qualifications, — perhaps more rare
than either of these, — tact and common
sense; and so he had, hitherto, only watched
and waited, prayed and trusted. In the
meanwhile, he was the frequent, and ever
welcome, guest at Mr. Chauncey's house
and table. And, whether he was talking
business or politics with the gentlemen, or
interesting himself in the girls' pursuits, or
helping Frank in some of his studies, or en-
tertaining the little ones with stories of his
boy-life, in the Maine woods, he was con-

sidered a friend by each one, and loved and respected accordingly. And, though he had spoken to them but few personal words, his trumpet gave no uncertain sound. His influence was most manfully exerted on the side of " Whatsoever things are pure." And the Chaunceys all felt that he was a true Christian; and in their inmost hearts, perhaps, they sometimes had a half-formed longing to know that peace which kept his brow unruffled through great sorrows; that source of strength which was, apparently, inexhaustible.

CHAPTER VI.

Two weeks rolled by as rapidly as time always does travel. And, on Wednesday morning, Margaret was to leave for New York, in company with the president of the college. It had been a busy fortnight, and had been, for the most part, filled with pleasurable anticipations, though Margaret's heart, once in a while, misgave her, at the thought of being so long away from the dearest ones on earth. Over and over again had she talked with Emily about her influence in her uncle's family; many times had

she prayed for strength to let her light so
shine before them that her Father should
be glorified. On Monday evening, when
most of her preparations had been completed — for her methodical mind had, from
the first, planned matters so as to leave
Tuesday free for visits and farewells — the
twilight hour found Margaret with her father
and mother, in the library, while the boys
had gone to a meeting of the college society,
to which both belonged. There was silence
at first, for the time of separation was
drawing near, and was pressing upon them
with its shady side foremost. But, after a
little while, Margaret said:

"Father, there is one thing I have been
thinking about a great deal, since this visit
was decided upon; and that is, amusements."

She paused, hoping that at the mere mention of the word her father would take the

lead in the conversation.   But he only said:

"Well?"

And she asked:

"What stand ought I to take in regard to them?"

"What amusements do you mean?"

"O, the mooted ones, of course! Dancing, cards, billiards, the opera, etc.   Am I, unhesitatingly, to decline participating in them, or what am I to do?"

"What do you wish to do?"

"Indeed! that is just my difficulty.   I do not know enough about them to pass judgment on them.   The general feeling here is so decidedly against them all, that I share the prejudice, if prejudice it be; and yet, I do not know that my impression is based on any reason."

"Well, dear, it seems to me that you are old enough to decide respecting these matters, yourself; and to have a reason, more-over, for your decision."

"I was pretty sure that you would say that; and I can see that it is right. But it would be far easier to limit my conscience to "Honor thy father and mother," and to refrain from anything doubtful at your advice, than to act independently. Yet, even if I did, I should want to be armed against the attacks of the world. Laughter and scorn may be endured silently; but argument must be met with argument."

"Do you anticipate collision on these points?"

"Why, sir, of course, more or less. You know the girls would think it very "Puritanical" in any one to refuse to participate in any one of the amusements I have named."

"Have you no definite opinion about any of them?" asked her mother.

"I don't think I have, really definite. I can see many objections to the theatre; some to the opera. Cards seem to me harmless, in themselves; but they do, very often, lead to gambling. I should think billiards must be a beautiful game. The round dances, I cannot imagine myself enjoying; but the difference between them and the square dances seems to me almost infinite."

"Is not one of the worst phases of all these amusements the fact that they consume so much time? that they are apt to be carried to excess?"

"I know that is one often brought forward, Mother, dear; but it does not seem to me a very good one. Is not too much of almost anything injurious? Would it be any more right to devote all one's life to study, even to the highest kind of intellectual self-cultivation, than to have one's mind full of nothing but dancing?"

"I think you are right, dear Mag. A medium point is generally the safe one about every occupation, except those which are wrong in themselves. The first question about these amusements is, — Are they wrong in themselves? The second is, — Would their effect upon me be injurious? And the third is, — How will they affect my influence? Make these your test questions, my daughter, and decide by them. So much it is but right that I should say to you; for the rest, I think it will do you more good to decide yourself. 'That ye keep yourselves unspotted from the world,' is the injunction; but, at the same time, we have to be in the world, and I firmly believe that every one must draw the line of demarcation for himself. Whichever way you may decide, I am sure you will not be left to yourself; and next to your best Friend, you have us. This matter seems likely to be a good deal in your mind, this winter; and the discipline will, undoubtedly, bear much fruit. I had thought of it before you spoke. And, my darling, I do not think your mother and I could have sent you out into the world if we had not first seen you putting on ' the whole armor of God.' "

The tears, which many times that day had come very near the surface of Margaret's eyes, overflowed, for a moment, at these last words; and she was glad to sit in silence for a little while. She was in her favorite seat, in the bay window; and, as the moon rose above the tree-tops, and cast a flood of soft light across the village green, and into the library, it seemed to lend new witchery and beauty to the places she loved

so well. There were not many more words
spoken till the boys came in.

"What a glorious night!" said Rob,
dashing over to Margaret's side. "Don't
you think you are hard-hearted, deliberately
to turn your back on all this loveliness, and
shut yourself up among the stones and
bricks of the city?"

"Sour grapes!" said Walter, quietly.
"Who said, last week, he wished he could
go to some large place for a while?"

"So I would. I'd like to settle in New
York, I admit. But not on account of the
place; only because it is one of the business
centres of the country. I should like to be
in business there, and to live, — say, on the
Hudson, somewhere."

"And yet, it is a grand place. There are
such great big hearts there; such large opportunities for doing good," said Walter.

"Deacon Ward would think you very

blind, if he heard you say, there were big hearts in New York, Walter," said Margaret.

" Oh! I know he thinks ' city ' and ' crime ' are synonymous terms. But I don't think you would want me to model all my ideas after his, if he is such a good man."

" No, indeed! And I quite agree with you. An upright, Christian, New York merchant seems to me one of the noblest of men. And I should not object to seeing one of you boys settled there."

" Then, look out for a good opening for me; and, when I have my diploma, pronouncing me a liberally-educated man, I'll see what I can do there," said Rob.

" Well, children, Mag will have a tiresome day to-morrow. I think we had better have prayers now," said Mrs. Worthington. So they drew around the table, when Walter had lighted the lamp, and after a hymn, they read in alternate verses the fourth chapter of Philippians. Margaret's voice had a thrill in it as she read: "My God shall supply all your need according to his riches in glory by Christ Jesus." It seemed to her a pledge that she would not be left alone in any perplexities that might arise in her life in the great city. Her father's prayer seemed more fervent than usual, even; and such a subdued feeling stole over her of perfect rest and serenity in the "everlasting arms," that her rest, that night, was unbroken as a child's.

CHAPTER VII.

Tuesday morning's sun shone bright and clear, and Margaret sprang up with delight that her last day at home should be such a beautiful one. The sunshine was contagious, and all was mirth and merriment around the breakfast-table.

"What are your plans for the day, Mag?" at last asked her father.

"Visits, principally, sir. I am going to make the rounds and say good-bye to every one. Emily is going with me."

Soon after breakfast they started, and

scarcely a house was passed by unentered. The interest felt by every inhabitant of a small place in every other inhabitant, is very pleasant; and Margaret was such a special favorite that her departure, for several months, was no small matter in the eyes of the Rowenah world. Various were the farewell words which were spoken. Various the expressions of good will; but Mag knew that they all came from the hearts of the speakers, and she reciprocated, fully, the feelings which prompted them.

"I think I will go to your house last of all, Em," she said. "I want to see your father and mother as short a time before I leave as possible; and as you are coming down to tea, I will wait, and go up there when you go home. Ah! here comes Deacon Wood. Mr. Wood, I have just been saying good-bye to Mrs. Wood and the children."

"So you're goin' to-morrow?   Wa'al, good-bye to you.   We'll miss you a good deal.   We're all used to seein' you round; and your singin' helped us along right powerful in the meetins, and at Sunday School. But young folks like change, and it's all right they should.   Only don't get so fond of New York that you'll be unwilling to come back to us again.   And, Marget, the city is a hard place to keep straight in. It's full of temptations and snares for the young, and Satan goes about like a roaring lion, seeking whom he may devour.   Stick to your principles, and don't budge an inch. You've always been a good child among us, here at home, but you don't know what you're going into, now."

"There is no danger of my ever loving any place so well as dear old Rowenah, Mr. Wood.   I have too many good friends here for that to be possible; and as to the rest, don't you think, sir, that strength will be given equal to my day?"

"I hope so, I hope so. But we must all be watchful. It's a bad thing to be too confident; it makes us more apt to fall. Young people are too apt to think they cannot be moved. But I hope the Lord will sustain ye. My Lizur thinks you can't do no harm, anyhow, or anywhere; and I must say, she's been a better girl at home since she was put into your Sunday School class."

"I am very glad that you see an improvement in her, sir; but now I must run on, for I have ever so many other people to see. Good-bye, sir."

"Good-bye, Margaret. You don't look like a girl to forget old friends. The Lord bless ye."

"What a pity it is that that man never had an opportunity to enlarge his views about matters and things in general,'' said Emily, as they passed on. "He is so good, and so friendly, and so large hearted; and yet, in some things so narrow minded."

"I know it. The boys were talking, last night, of his horror of a city life, and his unwillingness to believe that any good could come out of New York. It is so strange. Now, shall we go in there?" They had reached the little house where a modest sign announced that the Misses Emmons were "Fashionable Milliners and Dress Makers." They were much more than that sign announced. And perhaps a city modiste would have laughed at the adjective fashionable. They plied their respective trades briskly, and managed, by hook and by crook, to gain a living for themselves and their aged father. But their business was by no means their life. They were the village factotums in all times of sickness and distress; and their little parlor had been the scene of all sorts

of confidences poured into their ears by all
who appreciated the worth of their true
hearts. A cozy little snuggery it was, on
this cool morning, with a bright little wood
fire crackling on the open hearth, and on
the shining andirons; and it seemed hard to
say which shone the brightest, the sunshine
which streamed over the floor from the
windows, or the heart-sunshine within, as
the elder sister, Miss Chryssie, advanced,
with both hands outstretched, to welcome
the girls.

"There, sit down, girls, and I'll call
Harriet. I said, this morning, I was sure
you would be dropping in to-day," and she
disappeared for a moment. "Well, well,
we shall miss you, Margaret: but it's a fine
chance for you, and will do you good. I
never shall forget my visit to New York!
I was even younger than you are now; and
there were no railroads, and the journey was

more of an affair than a trip to Europe is now-a-days. I never knew, before, that the world was so big; and it was like a long fairy story all the time I was there. I stopped with friends in Pearl street. They say it's all built up with stores, now; and we used to walk on the Battery, and that's where the emigrants come in now, they say. You won't see the same New York that I did, Margaret; but you can enjoy the new more than I did the old, and I am glad you are going. I would like to go myself again; and I often say to Harriet, — here she comes ! "

" Good morning, Miss Harriet. Miss Chryssie says she would like to go to New York again. I don't see why you don't take a trip there, some day."

" To New York ? Ah ! no, Margaret. New York is not the place for old ladies like ourselves. Our friends have either died or moved away, and there is not a corner to spare there for us. There are some things there that I should like to see; but, it would be a sad sort of face I should carry around among the great sights. For our Charley, our own boy, wandered away there, you know, and forget his old aunties, who would have died to save him, body or soul."

The girls had heard the sad story of the fall of the wayward youth, the only son of an only sister of these ladies, — yes, ladies, girls, though they were milliners! ladies of more refinement than many a butterfly of fashion! — orphaned in his infancy, and brought up by his aunts, only, alas! to fill their cups almost to overflowing with sorrow. They remembered the sad days when Miss Chryssie had shut herself up alone, and refused to listen to comfort; and when Miss Harriet had come into church with bowed form, as one crushed. But the aunts themselves had never alluded to it before in their hearing. And now responsive tears of sympathy stood in all eyes, as Miss Harriet said:

"What I like best to think about in New York now, is the missionary work in the city, — the Christian associations, the reading rooms, the mission stations. I can't help thinking that if there had been more of these when our Charley went there, there would have been more chances of his keeping straight. Poor boy! he was so good-natured, always. He would go with any one who was kind to him. And there were so many to lead him astray. The billiard saloons and the theatres outnumbered the reading rooms and the church meetings; and there was no one to watch over him. I can't help feeling, yet, that we shall hear of him again, somewhere. And I pray for him just as often as I did while he was right here, at home; for we were never sure that he was dead. Margaret, could you send us word, sometimes, about the mission schools, and all that? The papers don't seem to say half I want to hear. And if you get a chance to do any good to boys who are growing up in the temptations of New York, remember our boy; and do your work all the more earnestly, because you have heard of him."

"Thank you, my dear Miss Harriet. I will." And she kissed the old lady's cheek. "Good-bye! You won't forget me, I know. And it is not only the boys who meet with temptations in the cities; so please help me along with your prayers," she whispered. "I have never had to depend on myself, you know. Good-bye, dear Miss Chryssie, — good-bye."

"Poor old ladies!" said both the girls, as they passed out. "Is it not strange, Em,

that they should mourn so over that scape-
grace, and yet, not strange, either, but
sad? Do you know it startled me to hear
Miss Harriet say that about billiard rooms
and the theatre? There is one strong argument against them."

"Yes, indeed. And do you know I
cannot get out of my mind what she said
about not believing him to be dead?"

"O, I think he must be, Em; it is so
long since they heard the rumor, since the
body was found in the river with his clothes
on, and the things in the pockets? I don't
think he can be living. And now for these
three houses in a row, and then Aunt
Dinah's, and then I may go home till I go
to your house." The three calls were soon
made, but Aunt Dinah's was a work of time.

"O honey! what's I goin' to do?" was
her salutation, while the tears ran down her
cheeks. "'Pears like I couldn't live with-

out seein’ you a-comin’ in the gate to read the Good Book to me.”

“Dear Aunt Dinah! I know you love me, and will miss me; but I shall think of you very often, and Miss Emily is coming to take my place whenever she can.”

“Miss Em’ly’s mighty good; but I want you, Miss Marget. I don’t mean no disrespecks to you, indeed, Miss Em’ly; but an old woman like me don’t like changes.”

“But I shall come back before a great while, Aunt Dinah. It will be only through the winter.”

“Ah, honey! Dinah’s rheumatiz was very bad last winter; and it may be de good Lord is gwine to take her home this year. And it do ’pear like I couldn’t die quiet ’thout you was alongside, reading the ‘many mansions.’ ”

“Aunt Dinah, I can’t bear to hear you talking so! I think you will live a long time yet, and will see me a great many more times; and if Jesus should take you home this winter, you won't need anything from me. You think too much of me. I am not half so able to help you along as Miss Emily is; and may be you will find that out for yourself."

"Chile, don't you say no such thing! The Lord sent you to me long ago, and you belongs to me. I know it's mighty selfish in me to talk this a-way, and that you's a-goin' to have no end of a good time, and I won't 'stress you no more. I said to myself this morning, 'Dinah, you mustn't complain. The Lord's done heaps better 'n you deserve already. And you mustn't make Miss Marget feel bad 'bout goin', when the Lord calls her." But when I see you comin' in at the gate, and knowed it was to say good-bye, I couldn't stan' it no longer."

And the old woman rocked back and forward in such genuine grief that Margaret hardly knew what to say.

"Aunt Dinah," at last she began, with her own voice full of grief, "I did not know you would feel quite so badly. I shall write to you sometimes, and Miss Emily will read the letters. And see here, what I have brought you. She drew out a likeness of herself in a pretty little frame, and stood it on Dinah's table. The old woman was very much touched and delighted, and looked at it for some time, till Margaret, seeing that she was quiet, rose to go. Dinah took both hands in hers and said:

"God bless you, dear Miss Marget, for all you've done for an old woman; but I must hear your voice jes' once more. Couldn't you take the time to read me the many mansions?"

"Certainly, Dinah!" and she took the

Bible. Dinah knew the chapter by heart, the words which have given life and refreshment to so many, and she followed as Margaret read, till the peace of the Spirit filled her soul, and the leave-taking afterwards was more calm than could have been hoped for. Dinah even half-apologized to Emily for the preference so strongly expressed, and thanked her for her willingness to take Margaret's place, and then said:

"Good-bye, dear chile. Have just as good a time as you want to, only keep near de blessed Jesus."

"I am afraid to try to fill your place, Mag," said Emily, as they went up the street.

"O Em, please don't say so! I am sorry you were with me, since it has made you feel so. I am sure Dinah will love you just as much as she loved me; and I hope she will be willing to see how much better you

are than I am. It frightens me to hear her
talk, and to feel conscious of having done
so little. Indeed, I am quite oppressed by
the affection every one expresses towards
me. I feel so undeserving ; and I cannot see
how I have gained so much love.''

" It is easy enough for others to see how
you do, dear ; and I don't think you ought
to let it distress you.''

" Distress is not the word. I rejoice in
it, and am thankful for it, as for one of
God's very best gifts. And although I
cannot help feeling that if people knew me
they would see how far below their idea of
me I really am, it does not make me want
to show them more of myself ; I am willing
they should be deceived in me. Is that a
horrible thing to say ? ''

" They are not deceived, Margery child.
Of course you have sins and short comings
in your heart that do not rise to the sur-

face; but the reason they do not is that you are able, by God's grace, to keep them down. If you let them all come up you would let them overcome you, instead of overcoming them."

" Do you remember that verse of Trench's? I so often think of it, —

'But friends might loathe us if what things perverse
We know of our own selves, they also knew, —
Lord, Holy One ! if thou, who knowest worse
Shouldst loathe us too ! '

If He loved us only for the good He could find in us, we should be poorly off, indeed. But, ' We love Him, because He first loved us.' ' While we were yet sinners Christ died for us.' And Maggie, I think it is so, in some measure, with human love; certainly with the love a Christian bears his friend. Of course the more Christ-like a person is, the more a person is drawn to him; but we love a great many people with very prominent faults. We love them, not even in spite of their faults, exactly; we love them just as they are. I always did contradict the assertion that love is blind. I think love has sharper eyes than any one else. We are painfully sensitive to the faults of a friend. Not because we come into collision with them, for we can overleap them. But because they influence the opinion of those who are not in circumstances to see the counterbalancing points which make us overleap them. It does not at all follow that all the people who love you so dearly, who admire you, think you faultless. I am sure you see faults in people; and yet, who loves her friends more dearly than you do? It would be arrogant and conceited, to say nothing of the impossibility of the thing, to wait for perfection before bestowing love on our fellows."

This conversation brought the girls to Mr. Worthington's gate, and Emily continued her walk homewards, renewing her promise of joining Margaret at tea-time.

" Well, here you are ! " was her mother's greeting to Margaret. " I have been watching for you for some time. Your Sunday School class is waiting in the parlor to see you."

" My girls ! Are they? Why, I have said good-bye to them all ! but I am glad they have come."   And she went in to see them.

" Well, girls, I am glad to see you again. How nice of you all to come together ! "

" Miss Margaret," said the eldest of them, the one who was generally spokesman, " we wanted to give you something to remember us by, and so we put our money together, and then we didn't know what to get. Some of us wanted to get a Bible, but Mother she said you had used your own for

so long she didn't believe you would want
to give it up; and we wanted you to use
what we gave you. So we couldn't think
what to get; but at last Susy's mother
said, wouldn't it be nice for each of us to
make you something our own selves. And
so we did, and here they are."

'O, thank you, girls! Yes, indeed, that
was a great deal better than to buy a present; tell your mamma I said so. Susie. O,
these are beautiful! pen-wiper, pin-cushion,
mats, book-mark, and needle-book. All so
pretty and so useful and so neatly made,
too. Thank you, over and over again. But
what is this?" as a folded paper showed
itself beneath the other things. The girls
hesitated and looked at each other, then at
Lizzie who, with some embarrassment, said:

"You see, Miss Margaret, we wanted to
remember what you said on Sunday, and
what you wanted us to promise; and so we

thought we would write it down and sign our names to it, and each take a copy and give you a copy, and so we did."

Margaret unfolded the paper and read:

" We promise our own dear teacher to read our Bibles every day, and to pray every day; to pray our own words, and try to do it from our hearts, and not just say our prayers; and to try to love the Saviour and be Christians.

ELIZA,

MAGGIE,

SUSIE,

JEANIE,

DORA."

" This is better than all the rest, girls; and I shall put the paper in my Bible and keep it there as long as I live. Now let us kneel down and ask Jesus to help us all to keep this promise." So they clustered around her, and a few words seemed to seal the promise and to be a pledge of strength for the future.

"You look tired, Margie," said her mother at the dinner-table.

"I think saying good-bye is dreadful work, Mamma; and Aunt Dinah's grief nearly upset me. But I shall feel refreshed when I have had dinner. I shall not go out again till after tea; we can have the afternoon to ourselves."

"How often do you mean to write to us, Margery?" said Rob.

"O, very often, of course! There is no danger on my side. I think the question is, Master Rob, how often you will deign to write to me? It strikes me you are not much of a scribbler."

"But I'll write to you, Marge, never fear, every other day, if you want me to."

"Take care, Rob," said his father. "Don't promise what you are not likely to perform. But my dear, suppose we manage a regular plan for correspondence. Suppose you write two letters a week; one week to your mother and Rob, and the other to Walter and myself. And each of us will answer his or her own letter in the week after it arrives. Will that be too great a demand upon your time, daughter? "

" No, indeed, sir; I shall like it. It will be very pleasant to know just what to expect. And my letters will be quite journal-like. I have not bid Mr. and Mrs. Robertson good-bye yet; but I believe I have seen every one else. I shall go up there after tea. Father, won't you be in New York, yourself, in the vacation? "

" I cannot tell. Possibly I may. I should like to spend a few days with you then."

*   *   *   *   *   *

The day wore away. Wednesday came. Mr. Robertson and Emily accompanied Prof. Worthington's family to the cars. Walter and Rob had stormed and hugged, Mrs. Worthington had held Margaret in a long clasp, as if she could not let her go. The trunks were checked, the lunch basket and satchel carefully arranged; the whistle had sounded; the group on the platform had watched the train till it disappeared around a curve, and Margaret was on her way to New York.

CHAPTER VIII.

"The train must have been late," said Kitty, as she wandered for the fortieth time to the window.

"Why no, dear; it is scarcely time for them to be here," answered her mother. "But the boys were as impatient as yourself, and rushed off early."

"Here they come, at any rate." And Kitty darted to the door. "O Mag, you darling, come in quickly!"

"I suppose she may get out of the carriage first," said Fred, assisting his cousin, and coming up the steps with her.

" Saucy fellow! I'd box your ears, if I could let go of Mag."

" Margaret, dear, I am so glad to see you," said Aunt Alice. And Laura took a long satisfied look as she sat down close to her cousin. Mr. Chauncey and the boys came in immediately, and the little ones followed soon. And no one could doubt the warmth of the welcome which Margaret received.

" Are you tired, Mag? " said Kitty.

" Not a bit."

" Or hungry? "

" No; here is Mother's basket half full yet."

" We will have dinner soon, at any rate," said Aunt Alice. " Did you ask the Doctor to come with you, dear? "

" Yes; but he said that as he had seen

Mag safely in my hands he would go right to the hotel. He promised to dine with us to-morrow."

"Now, Laura, you had better take Mag up stairs and let her rest till dinner is ready, even if she will not admit that she feels tired. We have given you a room to yourself, Margaret," said Aunt Alice. "Laura said she did not believe you were timid, and we all thought it would be pleasanter for you to have a retreat of your own, though I believe Kitty had set her heart on never leaving you, day or night."

"It was very thoughtful in you, dear Aunt Alice. I always have slept alone, you know. But Kitty dear, I think you will see enough of me."

Up stairs the girls ran, and Margaret could not but exclaim at all the evidences of loving preparation that met her eye.

"You won't be homesick, Mag, will

you? " said Kitty, as Mag changed her dress and refreshed herself after her journey.

" Homesick? O, no indeed! I expect to be as happy as possible. Laura dear, it is ever so good to see you again."

Laura's old dread had come up unbidden as she stood there with her cousin; but at these words her arm stole around Mag, and she gave her a hearty kiss. " I expect we shall have glorious times together," and then, the dinner-bell ringing, they all went down stairs.

" Is your voice in good training, Mag?" said Fred.

" Very much as it always has been, Fred, if you call that good training."

" We have a splendid chorus class this winter, which just needs your alto to complete it. I hope you have brought all your songs."

" O yes, indeed! I did not venture to

come into your august presence without my
music. And indeed, I was not anxious to
leave it at home.”

“ The Philharmonics begin soon, and they
promise to be very fine this year. Won’t
we enjoy them together? ”

“ Very much, I am sure. I expect to
enjoy everything I see and hear.”

“ That’s right,” said Uncle Henry.
“ How is your mother this fall, Margaret? ”

“ O, very well indeed, sir! Able to do
everything and to go everywhere. She expects Cousin Charlotte to make her a long
visit soon; and that, you know, she always
enjoys.”

“ I wish Cousin Charlotte would come
here; but she seems to think New York is
at the Land’s End, and too far away from
home for her. I have some hopes of getting
her here yet, though.”

“ How much study are you ready for, Mag ? ” asked Kitty.

“ O any amount of it ! What are you doing ? ”

“ Well, we put off German till you should arrive. But we shall begin to-morrow, and we mean to work very hard at it.”

“ O, I am sorry you waited for me ; I could have managed to catch up with you.”

“ Of course you could. But it is much pleasanter to start all together, and it made no difference to Mr. Fluegel. He is to come on Mondays and Thursdays, at ten o’clock. In French, we are only reading, and pretending to talk a little. We felt that we really did not need to have a master any longer. We have made great resolutions about talking, and we do very well for about fifteen minutes, when we have nothing special to say. Then, something is started which demands animated conversation, and we relapse into our mother tongue. It is the same way in trying to talk to the children. We make excellent resolutions and spasmodic efforts, but Sue's "Qu 'est-ce que cela veut dire?" comes in so often that translating becomes burdensome, and — O here she comes! Come here, darling."

" O Cousin Mag! are you going to sit by me? I'm so glad. I was afraid you wouldn't to-night, 'cause I only come down to dessert. But you will to-morrow, and all the time, won't you? "

" There it is, you see," said Mr. Chauncey, laughing. " Sue has too much to say to limit her conversation to a few French phrases. And as to Arthur, — How is it with you, my boy? "

" Papa, you know I don't like French. If it were Latin, now, I might care to learn to speak it."

"O Art!" cried Kitty. "Imagine us all sitting here, rolling out Latin periods. We might as well be Sir Thomas Mores, or Dr. Johnsons, at once."

"I used to go on just so about French, Art," said Fred, "though I did not like Latin any better. But I tell you, you'll be sorry enough some day, if you don't learn French. I felt as stupid as an owl when we first went abroad and I had only school-boy French, and precious little of that, at my command; while the girls could jabber equally well with porters and ambassadors. Besides, if you go into business, you'll find every modern language just so much extra capital, while the dead ones make but a sorry show on Wall street."

"You don't mean to say, though, that you think Latin and Greek useless," said Mag.

"No, I don't say that. I think every one

ought to learn Latin as a foundation for the modern languages, if for no other reason. I didn't think so when I had to learn it. And because no knowledge is admitted to be useless, I think Greek may as well form a part of a gentleman's education, always providing he can get the hang of it. I never could. I must say I do not see that it is ever of any practical service to any one out of a professor's chair. I am sure mine has never done me any good. And I do say, Mag, begging pardon of your father, the Greek professor of the family, that, in this country, and in these times, if it came to a choice between the dead languages and the living, I would say, study the living, especially to a boy who had his own way to make in the world. You have no idea of the intercourse with foreigners in our business life now-a-days. We meet men of every nation, and especially Germans. And even those who understand English will put a great deal more confidence in a man who can speak to them in his own tongue."

"Perhaps you are right," said Margaret, thoughtfully. "But I never realized all this before. Do you agree with Fred, Frank?"

"In a measure," said Frank, "not altogether. That is, I love the study of classics too well to see it under-rated without wanting to take up the cudgel in its defence. Still, I do appreciate what Fred says about modern languages; and that, not only in business life, but in the professions, too, — the lawyers, at any rate. I have often heard lawyers say that they lost a good deal of business because of their ignorance of that language. And I like a collegiate education, myself."

"I am glad there is one defender of the old faith," laughed Margaret.

8

" The dust of classic halls still clings to your feet, eh, Mag? "

" I suppose so, Uncle Henry. I suppose it is because I have been brought up in a college town, and among students, that a collegiate education has always seemed to me necessary, or I ought rather to say thoroughly desirable, for a gentleman, though, — " and she glanced at Fred.

" Yes! I knew you thought me somewhat of a natural curiosity, and were not quite sure whether I ought to be sent to Barnum's Museum or to the lunatic asylum, when I deliberately chose Wall street instead of Yale. But I couldn't help it, and I am not sorry yet. Here is Frank, now. He don't care how many hours he spends digging Greek roots, which would drive me crazy as soon as, — well, as soon as the Gold Room or the Board of Brokers would make his brain reel."

Frank laughed and said: "Business would never suit me, that's certain. And although Fred is a fair specimen of a fellow without a college education, I don't think his theories are all right. There are some New York boys who go down town direct from the nursery, and the consequence is, that they have no more ideas in their heads than a pin has, except in the mere matter of business. They manage to get through a routine there, very much like a spoke in a machine, with about as little free-will as it has. They know the fashionable tint for gloves; they are connoisseurs in cigars and in 'girls;' but as to 'thinking a thought,' as Kit used to say when she was little — bah! I can't help despising them."

"Yes," Laura said. "Fred, you know, Mag, always had a way of picking up information. I don't believe he ever studied real hard in his life till he took up French after feeling the want of it, but he always kept his eyes open. He read a good deal, when he could get the kind of reading he liked. But he observed a great deal more. So, because he can't help feeling that he knows more than some men who have been to college, he has this way of ranting. For my part, I think the amount of it is this. A boy who loves learning for its own sake, really loves to study, ought to go to col-lege; and a boy who doesn't care to do that, had better go down town. There are men who come out of college with no more ideas than those whom Frank has been be-rating. Even college don't supply brains; it only expands such as are already fur-nished. Why not let a boy's own choice decide these matters, rather than general principles or fashions?''

"That might do well enough," said her father, "if there were not a great many idlers and weather-cocks who would never decide upon anything, and if it made no difference to a boy how fast he got on pecuniarily. I have seen cases where it has been very hard to know what was best to do; and some where, apparently, the best had not been done. There is Charley Seymour; he went to college and did pretty well for a couple of years, and then circumstances made it advisable for him to go into business. He did so, and is doing finely, without seeming to pine for his books; while Mr. Wardlaw looks like a man who has made a great mistake. He was born to be a student, and business life is clearly not his forte at all, though he went into it conscientiously, for the sake of his family."

" Is not the trouble often, Uncle Henry, the making haste to grow rich? Are there not some who could make fine scholars if they chose, whose eyes are so blinded by

the desire to have money that they will not
wait? I mean those who could wait, as well
as not. And in the other case, could not
rich men often do a great deal of good by
helping young men through college? I don't
mean by founding a scholarship for any one,
but by finding out some individual and giving him aid quietly, so that he shall not feel
himself a beneficiary of an institution, and
delicately, so that he need not feel himself
a burden? "

" Is not that rather a Quixotic scheme,
Mag? "

" If it is, sir, I think it is a sad reflection
upon human nature and upon the state of
feeling of the present day. If it is more
blessed to give than to receive, people ought
to find it out; and receiving surely ought
not to be considered a disgrace. If God
has put some in a position to give, and
others in a position to receive, each party

has its duties, and I do not think they ought
to clash."

"Well, then, Broker Fred, if Student
Frank ever gets into difficulties you must
help him out," said Kitty.

"I hope I should; but Mag is not talking about brothers."

"I'm not so sure, either, Fred, — though
I really don't know statistics to prove my
position,—that in the long run those who have
chosen a mercantile life have had the greatest
pecuniary success. Have they?"

"I don't know. You think that it may
some day be Judge Frank's turn to help
poor Fred out of a scrape. I shouldn't
much wonder, if gold speculations go on all
our days. Nobody who gets into these
knows where he will land. I think, — "

"I think you have all talked long enough
about this," said Aunt Alice, rising from
the table. "Susie, at least, finds it stupid,

and Mag ought to be too tired to discuss
such deep matters."

" Mag has evidently thought a good deal
about the matter, at any rate," said Uncle
Henry, " and the subject is not easily exhausted.   But now, Susie, do you want a
romp ? "

" O yes, Papa; please dance."

" Dance, Sue ! is not Papa too old for
that ? "

" No indeed, Papa; nor ever will be.
Please, Kitty, play."

A lively tune soon satisfied Sue, and the
spirit was contagious. Fred seized Laura,
and Frank came up to Mag with an affect-
edly ceremonious bow and " May I have the
pleasure, Miss Worthington ? "

Mag drew back, and Aunt Alice said:

" Do have some mercy on your cousin,
Frank. Think of the journey she has ac-

complished to-day, and the discussion she has been through now."

Mag laughed and said : "Neither of these would deter me, Frank, but you know I am only a country girl, and do not know one step from another. I never danced in my life."

"You don't know how to dance, Margaret Worthington! I was never more amazed in my life. Fred," — as Laura and Fred careered down the long parlor, — "Fred! come and see a natural curiosity. Mag doesn't know how to dance."

"Doesn't she?" She shan't say that very long. I'm a capital dancing master, Mag; come here and try me. One, two, one, two, come."

"No, thank you, Fred; I would much rather look on. You must not ask me, indeed."

"No; but I cannot do it."

"Don't bother her, Fred," said Kitty. "Here, Laura, take my place; I must have one galop."

"Well then, Mag, I'll let you off this time; but only this time, remember that."

She was left in peace on the sofa by her aunt, who took her hand caressingly, saying, "It's a real treat to have you here, Margie dear, and I hope you will be willing to stay a long time. Now tell me all about home; what are the boys about?"

"Studying hard, Auntie. And between whiles playing all sorts of pranks on us all. They are real mischief-lovers, and do not outgrow their boyhood at all."

"They like college?"

"O yes, indeed; and would not be willing to be anywhere else."

"What do they mean to do after graduating?"

"I do not feel certain. Walter is a

thorough student, and will study some profession. We often think that he may decide upon the ministry."

" Would you like that? "

" O yes, indeed! we all hope for it. But at the same time we feel that it is a thing which should come spontaneously, and, therefore, we do not urge it."

" But, Margaret, it is a life of great sacrifice and care and labor, and very, very little compensation."

" So it is, Aunt Alice. It is the last profession to attract one, viewed from a worldly stand-point. And yet, there is something so glorious about it — oh! we would be glad to see Walter choose it."

" And Rob? "

Mag laughed. " Rob is doing well in his class; but it is partly from family pride, and partly to please Father and Mother. I don't think he really loves study for its own sake.

I think he would like, better than anything
else, to come here and go into business.
He is thoroughly practical, and I should
think he would make a good business man.
The boys are so unlike. We often look at
them, and think that one would complete
the other. Walter is quiet and thoughtful,
tender as a woman, but perfectly outspoken
when principles are concerned. Well, they
are alike in that. But Rob is as impulsive
and impetuous as a little child. Everybody
loves Rob. He seems to belong to the whole
village. Children are devoted to him, and
he is a great favorite with the college boys.
Walter is apt to be very reserved. You
have to know him a good while to find out
what he really is. But when you have once
gained his friendship, you have it forever.
Dear old Walter! he is so good to me."

"Is he your favorite, then?"

"Favorite! O Aunt Alice, I do not think

I feel the least preference for one above the other. But I do feel that in a year or two more I shall find myself looking up to Walter as if he were older than I. Even now I go to him for advice sometimes. And when he sits down to talk over a matter, you would think him an old man, he is so mature. He is a man in a great many of his feelings, while Rob is nothing but a boy."

"Our boys are unlike, too. But the cases are reversed. Frank, although the younger, is more mature in thought than Fred, though Fred prides himself very much on being a man of the world. He is a great society man, — the girls all seem to like him." And Aunt Alice's eyes rested proudly on her handsome eldest boy. "Frank loves his book, and though he enjoys a good dance, I think he would rather take it at home than go to a party in search of it. Well, Susie, have you danced enough?"

" Yes, Mamma, I'm pretty tired; but Art wouldn't let me stop till I had danced with him."

" Do your brothers all pet you, Susie? " asked Cousin Mag. " Why yes, 'course they do," was the naive answer.

" And what do you do for them? "

" O I just loves them, that's 'bout all. Sometimes I get a flower from the 'servatory to put in Fred's button-hole when he's going to a party, and sometimes I run and get Frank's slippers, and Art sends me down stairs sometimes."

" Yes, she's our little messenger," said Frank, snatching her up. " See here, Missy, I don't think I've had a real hug to-night; suppose you let Cousin Mag see how you can squeeze.' '

The child did not need urging; and for the next fifteen minutes she was going from one to another, distributing her favors as impartially as possible, and finally, when Nurse claimed her, going off to bed, the veriest sunbeam of a darling · that ever was petted by a whole tribe of brothers and sisters.

The rest of the evening was spent quietly. Margaret, though unwilling to confess it, was beginning to feel a good deal tired, with her journey, and the excitement of the evening, and she was not sorry when they separated for the night.

In her own room she tried to think quietly of all the events of the day, but she could not but revert with a troubled feeling to the surprise her ignorance of dancing had aroused. "What shall I do?" said she. "What stand ought I to take? O I wish I knew what to do!" Then her aunt's words, "Fred prides himself on being a man of the world," came to her. "I shall have ridicule and sneering to bear from Fred," thought she, "and that will be hard. Still

I could do it, I suppose, if I were only sure
about the right stand-point. But the question is, where to yield, and where to hold
back? Fred is a winsome fellow; I want him
to like me. And oh! what joy it would be
if I could help him to become a Christian.
What a noble one he would make. How
strange it is that they should all be so lovely,
and yet not that. How careful I must be!
I wonder if the boys know that I am a
Christian? I did not feel very brave to-
night, when Frank was talking. I said I did
not know how to dance, and that is true;
but I did not say a word about principles.
That's the trouble. I don't believe I have
any principle in the matter. I'm sure I don't
see what harm there can be in dancing as
they did to-night. I would not like a
stranger to have his arm around me — I
wouldn't let him. But Fred and Frank —
why they hug and kiss me when they choose,

and I don't mind it from them any more than from Walter and Rob; so why not dance with them? There it is, though! If I dance with them, I can't say I don't dance; and if I can't say that, what can I say? O dear! not twenty-four hours away from home, and in a dilemma already. I wish I had Em here, or Father." As she said these words the verse stood out before her mind, " There is a friend that sticketh closer than a brother." " He is here," thought she, " and He always will be. 'My beloved is mine and I am His.' I was not trusting Him. He will help me. He will show me the right way, I do believe. 'Commit thy way unto Him.' So I will. How faithless I have been." And prayer calmed her. When does it not? And sleep soon banished all doubts and difficulties for the night.

9

CHAPTER IX.

" May I come in, Cousin Mag? "

It seemed to Mag that she had just fallen asleep, and she was bewildered by the sunlight and the strange room. But there was the little voice, irresistible in its appeal. Susie was making herself heard.

" Yes, dear; come in, of course. Why, are you all dressed? is it time to get up? "

" Pretty near. I have been waking up Laura and Kitty. But Laura said she wanted one more nap, and Kitty she say ' Run away, Susie dear,' so I came to see you."

Margaret laughed, and was holding out her arms to help Susie up on the bed, when Nurse appeared with a comical expression of disturbance, vexation, and apology on her face.

"Susie, Susie! come here, and don't be troubling your cousin. Indeed, Miss, I beg your pardon, and I should have been more careful; for Mrs. Chauncey said you were not to be disturbed after your journey. But my back was just turned, and I thought she had gone to the young ladies' rooms till I heard her calling you."

"O never mind, Nurse. I feel nicely rested; and I would much rather get up in season for breakfast. Is it most time for that?"

"It'll not be for three-quarters of an hour yet, Miss. So you can have another nap yet. Come, Susie."

"O, I am quite wide awake now, Nurse;

so please leave Susie here.   I like to have
her ; indeed I do."

" Well, Miss, if you please.   You'll not
be troublesome, Susie?"

" No, no," said little Susie.   " I'll be
real good, Nursie.   Go away, and let me
help Cousin Mag get dressed."

" Come here, then, and give me a kiss
before I get up, Sue."

Nothing loth, little Sue clambered up on
the bed, and nestling close to her cousin
said :

" This is the way I do to Kitty, when
she isn't too sleepy.   I like it ever so
much."

" I like it, too.   I never had any little
sisters to pet."

" Didn't you?" and Susie's eyes were big
with amazement.

" No ; only two big brothers like Fred and

Frank. But, Sue, tell me what you do with yourself all day long?"

" O, most everything. I say my lessons, sometimes."

" Do you? What lessons do you say?"

" O, A B C, and little spelling words, and twice one, that's all. When I get bigger, I'm going to have a lady come and teach me; and when I get real big, I'm going to school."

" Do you think you'll like that? "

" O yes! it's real fun to go to school; Kitty says so."

" Who teaches you now? "

" O Mamma or Laura or Kitty. Arthur tries sometimes; but I don't like him to, 'cause he ain't so very big. He says I ought to know what I don't know, and he gets mad at me."

" Not very mad, I guess. But what else do you do besides lessons? "

“O I play. I play with my dolls ever so much. O Cousin Mag! I’m going to bring my French doll here.’’ And while she tripped away to get it, Mag got up and began to dress.

“O, did you get up? Well please look here? ”

“Dear me! What a beauty! Is this your pet? ”

“Well, this is my company doll. I don’t play with her very often, ’cause she’s my Paris doll. I like to look at her, and show her to people; and she’s got lots and lots of clothes. But I’d rather have my Josey.’’

“And who is Josey? ”

“Oh! she’s my own old doll. She isn’t as pretty as Lina, ’cause she used to be Kitty’s, and she’s rather worn out. But I take her to bed, and I do all sorts of things to her. Sometimes she’s very bad; and I put her in the corner and say, ‘ Stay there till you're good, Miss.' And then she falls flat down, and I pretend she's screaming in a passion. And you know, if I let Lina fall, she'd break her nose; but Josey's nose is only rags."

"Have you got many story-books?"

"Yes, a good many. Papa gave me the Night Caps for my birthday. Have you ever read them? They're real funny. Papa laughed at them ever so much; and Arthur can say the story about the boy that was sent to market without looking at the book. One of the books is about West Point. We went there last summer."

"What did you see there?"

"O ever so many things. So many soldiers and guns and houses. The soldiers looked real nice, but I was afraid of them. Are you all ready, Cousin Mag?"

"Not quite, dear. But you may run down

now, or you may stop talking for a few moments, and wait for me."

"I'd rather wait." And she sat on a little stool as Mag knelt beside her bed. When she arose, Susie said:

"Do you say 'Now I lay me,' and 'Our Father?' I thought only little girls said that."

"Everybody doesn't use the same words, dearie. But every one ought to pray to God, you know."

"I don't believe Nurse ever says her prayers."

"Now, in a few moments more I'll be ready. But be quiet a little while yet."

The Bible opened at the twelfth chapter of Hebrews, and the first verses seemed like an inexhaustible store-house of grace and strength. "The cloud of witnesses looking unto Jesus." "Father, keep these words in my mind," she prayed, "and then I shall be prepared against the assaults of the enemy."

"Now, Sue, I'm ready; and there's the bell."

Susie hesitated, and in a moment said:

"Do Laura and Kitty say their prayers?"

"Why yes, dear, of course; I suppose so," Mag answered, a deal shocked by the question.

"Well, I never saw them," said Sue, "and I'm going to ask them."

"O no, Susie, I wouldn't," said Mag. "Here they come," as they went into the hall.

"Why, Margery, ready for breakfast? I thought you had the privilege of sleeping as long as you chose, to-day."

"I did sleep as long as I chose," Mag answered, kissing Kitty. "I am perfectly rested, and Sue has been helping me with all her might."

"Sue! Has she been with you? I drove her away from my side."

"So she said." And Mag laughed, adding, as Susie ran ahead, "What a chatter-box she is?"

"Yes, indeed; you must not let her torment you."

"O she doesn't. I enjoyed her visit ever so much. Children are a great novelty to me, you know."

"Yes," said Laura, who had joined them. "But Papa says we have spoiled Sue by letting her engross too much of our attention. She is real bright and cunning, and her remarks are often so pat that we encourage her to talk a good deal — too much, perhaps. The baby of a large family is always spoiled, they say. Why, are we the first down? Papa, only see; we are all ahead of you, to-day."

"All, my daughters, eh?" and Mr. Chauncey gave each one a good-morning kiss.

"Well, Margie, how are you,—rested?"

"O yes, indeed, sir."

"Well, Mamma," as Mrs. Chauncey appeared, "let's have breakfast; it is after eight, and we must be off, eh, Fred! We business men have to be very prompt."

"Yes, sir; but not more so than these ravenous school-boys. We eat breakfast on a rush here, Madge; that is, we masculines. I won't pretend to say how long the ladies sit here after we leave."

"Now, Fred, don't assume the magnificent, and pretend that we have nothing to do. If we do eat in a more civilized manner, we don't complain of dyspepsia, as I

have heard a certain young man do," exclaimed Laura.

" Besides," said Kitty, " don't you know
that

> Man's work lasts till set of sun,
> But woman's work is never done.

" I don't think man's work is finished at
set of sun, when he has to lead the German," growled Fred.

" O Fred! The idea of calling that
work."

" Well now, is it not? Jolly kind of
work, of course. But I'll be hanged if it
doesn't tire me as much as anything I have
to do. Don't you girls have to take bouillon
to help you through it?"

" There, Margie," said her aunt, " what
do you think of that kind of pleasure? "

" Pretty exhausting, I should think, Aunt
Alice."

“ But fascinating, at the same time, I assure you, Mag. I’m quite willing to stand the fatigue.’’

“ O, I don’t doubt it, Fred.’’

“ And you’ll be as eager about it as any of us, before long.”

“ I don’t think I will trouble the German much, Fred. I’m a real country girl, you know.”

“ Country nonsense! Beg your pardon, Mag. But you’re not a country girl at all. A country girl is a dowdy. fussy, prim Miss Nancy, who rolls up her eyes and primps everlastingly. You’re not a country girl.’’

“ Fred, for shame!’’ said his father.

“ I resent the description, sir, and I warn you not to repeat it. Country girls are not all alike, any more than city girls. And I am a country girl.”

“ My dear cousin! I had no intention of offending you. I meant to compliment you.

You are not dowdy; you are not fussy; you are, — ''

" Be still, sir," said Mag, " or I shall go back to my native hills where, at least, I can venture an opinion without being scorned for it."

" The war of words has begun," said Frank. " I never saw two people like you. You cannot leave each other alone."

" A truce to it now, at any rate," said Mr. Chauncey, " for I want to hear something definite about studies. To-day, you say, Herr Fluegel comes."

" Yes, Papa, at ten o'clock."

" And you are all to begin German together. Do you know anything of it, Mag? "

" Not a word, sir."

" And what book are you to use? "

" Ahn, sir, I believe."

" Mondays and Thursdays, then, you have

that. Now, about music. Mag, you mean to take lessons? "

Mag hesitated.

" Don't be afraid to speak, my dear. You are my daughter this winter, you know."

" You are too good, Uncle Henry. I have heard the Conservatory, lately, very highly recommended; and I thought perhaps I would go there. The terms are low, and it is said the instruction is admirable."

" Indeed! I know very little about it. What have you heard?"

" Prof. Goldwin's daughter spent some time here with her grandfather, last winter, and took lessons during her visit. She was thoroughly satisfied with the instruction, and certainly improved rapidly. They teach in classes, and Mattie thought the drill, in respect to time, particularly beneficial."

" Well, it may be worth while to go over

there and make inquiries.   But I want it
distinctly understood that all your tuition
comes upon my shoulders.''

'' But Uncle Henry, — indeed, — ''

'' Not a word, Mag.   It will not hurt
me, and I want to do it.   It is nothing to
what your mother did for me when we were
children.   Your father's allowance you will
find plenty of use for, I do not doubt.
There are more ways of spending money
here than Rowenah even dreams of. "

This was but an instance of Mr. Chauncey's dealing with Margaret throughout the
entire winter.   He treated her emphatically
as he promised, '' As his own daughter, "
and her visit was one unbounded pleasure
and improvement.   Lessons, concerts, lectures, paintings, all were enjoyed, and enjoyed to the utmost, as were also all sorts
of social gatherings at her uncle's house,
and at the houses of his numerous friends —

many of whom welcomed her, at the outset, for the sake of her parents, — all of whom soon learned to covet her society for their own sake.

10

CHAPTER X.

After breakfast on Thursday, Mag's first undertaking was her letter home,-- a bright, cheery description of her journey and her welcome, her cousins and their plans, overflowing with anticipations, and yet not unmingled with regrets. Not quite homesick, but just this :

" If you were only here with me, every one of you. Papa, how it would rest you. Mamma, you would take such thorough comfort in being constantly with Uncle Henry and Aunt Alice. While as for you, boys,

you would revel in everything. I am going
to have a real treat. I see it plainly. What
if it should spoil me? I ask myself this in
soberness, almost in anxiety, perhaps a little
faithlessly. You will all help me, with your
letters, to keep in the straight path; to be
vigilant; to be ' A living example known
and read of all men.' Amidst all the sunshine of this house I cannot but be impressed with the sad conviction — ' God is
not in all their thoughts.' I believe I never
before saw a day begun or ended without
family worship, — for when I made my other
visit here you were with me, Papa, and you
remember you asked Uncle Henry to let you
have it, — and I did not know, till now, how
much I valued it or should miss it. And
I could almost hear your voices, this morning, and feel that you missed me; that you
appreciated the difficulties of my position,

and that it would be through your prayers that I should conquer, if conquer I may."

The letter despatched, the first German lesson came. And after that, unpacking, "getting settled," as Kitty said.

"Now, Mag, you are really at home," when the last dress was hung, the last book laid on its shelf. "What books have you there? Did you think we could not furnish you?"

"No, indeed. But there are some old favorites, of which one must have one's very own close at hand, you know."

"So there are. I have often felt that. May I look?"

"Certainly."

"Holy Living and Holy Dying," "Mind and Words of Jesus," "Plain Words to a Young Communicant," "Hymns of the Church Militant."

Kitty made no comment, but there was a cloud on her face, and she turned uneasily away.

" What if — oh ! what if Laura were right after all, and Mag were spoiled by her religion.   How should she bear it ?   She loved Mag so dearly ! " But Susie's ringing laugh banished this train of thought, and Kitty turned, to find it occasioned by some of Mag's nonsense, produced for the child's entertainment.   And as the lunch-bell rang Susie's loving squeeze showed that she had not discovered any change for the worse in Margaret.   The day sped swiftly away. Callers and chatting and a walk filled the afternoon.   Dr. —— joined them at dinner, and music made the evening pleasant.   Old favorites among their glees and quartettes were brought forward, and one or two new ones tried.   The boys were in ecstasies. Fred declared Mag's voice better than ever, and a happier household it would have been difficult to find.

The next morning brought Mag her first letter from home; and while Fred bantered her, or tried to, by asking how Rowenah, with its little round of items, could, in forty-eight hours, produce material for the closely written pages, there was not a word that did not go right to Mag's heart.

" We miss you dear, all the time," her mother's portion closed. " But we are more than willing to miss you, for the sake of the pleasure you are having." But here the pen had evidently been seized by Rob, who thus relieved his mind:

" More than willing! Well, I suppose Mamma is. She always did love her children better than herself. Somehow, that sort of thing comes natural to mothers. But boys and brothers are made of another kind of stuff. Willing? May be I am. If ever a girl deserved a first rate time, my old Margery does.   And I rather guess I won't call you back.   But, O dear me! 'Things isn't what they used to was.'   'There's nae luck about the house since Margie went awa.' And the moral of all this is, Have the good time, just as much as you want to.   Only please don't forget that We, Us & Company are pining for letters, and none more so than

Your most obedient,

his
Rob W.   ×
mark.

Nobody would call this a great letter. But if boys wrote a few more like them, how their sisters would bless them.   It isn't any trouble, and if it were, isn't it worth while for the pleasure the letters give, and the warm feeling they keep up in the hearts of those whom necessity or circumstances separates?

This one was too characteristic to be lost,

so Mag passed it around, and all laughed heartily. Fred shrugged his shoulders.

"I say, girls, is that the way I ought to feel when you go off?"

"Wretch!" Kitty retorted. "You need not try to make us believe you are heartless."

"Rob has plenty of life in him, it seems," said Uncle Henry. "You say he is looking forward to a merchant's life?"

"Yes, sir, that is his desire."

"We must have him down here, then. There is plenty of room for boys of that kind."

"New York is his goal, sir," said Margaret; "though he will, of course, finish his college course first."

"A great mistake," said Fred. And the contest would have been renewed but for Mr. Chauncey starting for business, whither Fred had to follow him.

The week completed, Sunday came. Mag could but repress a little feeling of homesickness, at the thought of her boys and Aunt Dinah, but she struggled bravely against it, and in due time they started for church. Dr. Harris at once won her heart. He was simple, earnest, and persuasive, eminently practical, and very happy in his illustrations.

"I sometimes think," he said, to-day, " that there is one class of persons whom we do not sufficiently regard. I refer to young Christians. I do not mean youth alone, but persons, of whatsoever age they may be, who have lately begun to lead a Christian life. We labor with them before they make their decision ; we bear their burdens on our hearts to the mercy-seat; we pray for opportunities to speak the ' word in season ; ' we try to set before them Christ and Him crucified; we point out the way to the cross. And when they set their faces Zionward we give

thanks for them ; we welcome them to the
table of our Lord, and then we leave
them to themselves. Not always, perhaps,
but far too often, we forget that sanctification
is not like justification, — a momentary thing.
That the Christian grows just as a child
does, — slowly, although surely. That there
are slips in a Christian's life. That the
conscience, rendered doubly sensitive by the
responsibilities it has assumed, doubly eager
by the love that has been kindled, is also
a double mark for the adversary, who
watches, with a special jealousy, those on
whom the Lord hath set his mark. My dear
friends, — those whom it has been my privilege lately to welcome to the table of our
Lord, and any who may be in any of those
dark valleys into which our Father sometimes takes his children, let me beg of you
to share your trouble with some one who
may have had fuller experience than you in

tasting and seeing that the Lord is good. And O, my brethren, 'Take heed lest ye offend one of these little ones.' "

His sermon was upon Christians' helpfulness to one another. " Then they that feared the Lord spake often one to another," he quoted. And while he deprecated all cant, or talking in set formulas, and as a mere habit, he dwelt largely on the benefits to be derived from mutual confidences on this subject, and the necessity for laying aside, in a measure, the shrinking, prevalent among Christ's people, from speaking to one another of the things dearest to their hearts.

" Let your conversation be as becometh the gospel of Christ; comfort one another with these words," he said. "As a modern writer has asked, ' Why cannot the intercourse of Christians be Christian?' Between near and dear friends all other topics of mutual interest are freely discussed, while the one nearest to them is often the last one introduced; and then, with stammering or reserve or half-apology. My brethren, these things ought not so to be. Religion is a sacred thing, not to be flaunted in men's faces at all times; but it is also an every-day thing, to be the rule of our heart, and the law of our lives."

Margaret drank it in, and found it strength-giving; and could not but sigh as she thought of Emily, and the intercourse which must now be limited to letters.

In the afternoon her aunt and Laura and herself represented the family at church. Aunt Alice always went twice; Laura generally, perhaps because her knowledge of her pastor's look of disappointment when the pew was empty haunted her, and influenced her more than she would have cared to confess. Kitty plead a head-ache. Mr. Chauncey was asleep in the library, and Fred declared that once a day was enough for him. He joined them at the door, however, and urged Mag to stroll up the avenue with him, and looked a good deal disappointed when she declined.

"Too good for that? You know it's the only day you can have my society."

"I would rather go home, thank you, Fred. I'm just as much obliged to you."

"Don't apologize." But he turned off vexed, Mag could see, and sauntered away with Laura, while Mag went home with her aunt, very sober.

"This is the first attack," she was thinking. "O, what strength, what wisdom, I shall need! Suppose this should make me lose ground with Fred, when I so long to win him. Ought I to have gone? Perhaps there is no harm. Yet, all the time her heart told her she was right. And as the gay equipages rolled by, and the richly-dressed throng followed, she knew the comments some of them would have drawn forth from mirth-loving Fred, and she said to herself,

"It would have been thinking my own thoughts, and doing my own pleasure. And if I cannot win Fred, Jesus can."

It was a relief to her to get to her own room, and to steady and calm herself with prayer and with assurance from God's own word. And further, to commence a letter to Emily, full of all that had been on her heart through the day, and indeed week. And she was quite herself again when the tea-bell rang, and very glad to find that the fresh air had wafted away all Fred's displeasure, so that he was, apparently, as friendly as ever.

Fred was really very fond of Margaret, and he had quite counted upon her as a sharer in all his pursuits through the winter.

She was a cousin of whom he was justly proud. Her mental acquirements, her conversational powers, her voice, and her fine looks charmed him, and would, he knew, charm others. So he was eagerly looking forward to her appearance among their friends, along with his sisters. Her refusal of his first invitation had vexed, and even hurt him a little. But he was far from appreciating the fact that principle was involved, and attributed it to a sort of prejudice arising from her quiet life.

"They don't look at things quite through New York spectacles," he said. "But she will soon learn to do at Rome as the Romans do. They are a straight-laced set up there in the country. But she'll get over it. She's got too much sense to cling to such notions."

He did not speak of his disappointment to Laura. But she had seen all the proceeding, and it ruffled her more than it did

Fred, because she saw deeper into the matter. "It is going to be just as I feared," was her mental comment. "She will want to do differently from us, and perhaps to bring us round to her way of thinking. Dear me! she is so captivating. And yet she shan't preach to me. If she does, I'll lose every spark of affection for her, and I'll wish she had stayed away."

Yet even Laura could not resist the infection of the cheerful tea-table, and Margaret was so bright and affectionate, so good to the little ones, so charming with the boys, — Frank and she were great friends, — so like one of themselves with Kitty and herself, evidently a favorite with Mr. and Mrs. Chauncey, that Laura had to confess, "She isn't altogether spoiled. And if she only will keep her notions to herself, I guess there won't be any trouble."

CHAPTER XI.

Two or three weeks rolled by without any very striking events, or any occasion for conflict as to principles. Margaret was thoroughly domesticated in her uncle's household. Letters from home all brought good news, and she was very happy. Yet she foresaw questions looming in the distance which must, at least, cause her anxious thought; concerning which she would either have to yield prejudices instilled into her earliest childhood, or meet the enemy with a firm front. She did not put these aside

11

and wait in inaction till the crisis should come, but she fortified herself in the Christian's stronghold, putting on the armor of God, and confident of his care, endeavored not to be anxious overmuch. In the meantime, she was so bright and affectionate, so helpful and unselfish, so interested in the special pursuits of each one of the family, that her presence was a constant delight. Sue was her avowed champion, and perfectly devoted to her. Margaret had insisted upon undertaking to teach her, and the little girl enjoyed her regular lessons, and was soon making rapid progress on the high road to learning.

One Sabbath, about six weeks after her arrival, the Lord's Supper was to be celebrated. All the family but Fred were in church, but they all retired after the sermon, leaving Margaret alone in the pew. Her uncle looked at her with a little surprise, but made no comment as he left the church. Her aunt had already felt that there was some secret spring to Margaret's loveliness, and had felt that in her religion, at least, there was sincerity. The girls had, as we know, already discussed the stand she had taken. And Frank was about equally surprised and indifferent. Fred met them at the door of their house.

"Why, what have you done with Margie?" he asked.

"She remained in church," his mother answered. And Laura interrupted his question of amazement, by saying,

"It is Communion Sabbath, Fred, and Mag is a member of the church."

Her tone was strange, a little sarcastic, a little bitter, perhaps just a little mournful. She loved her cousin, and she did not want conscience to remind her that between them there was a great gulf.

Fred said nothing, but went back to the library.

"So this is what she means when she don't know how to dance, and won't take walks on Sunday. She's religious. Pshaw! there's an end of fun for the winter. But what possesses her? I thought old people and people who hadn't anything better to do, were the religious ones. I don't see what a pretty, bright girl wants of cant and all that sort of stuff. And yet she is not a bit gloomy. I told the girls, last night, she beat them all hollow for carrying on. It's beyond me. I guess it's just because she has always lived among that set of parson-professors up in the country."

His soliloquy was interrupted by his father.

"Fred," said he, "don't you want to walk over and meet your cousin?"

"Well, yes, sir, I have no objections;

that is, if you think she will care to come
home with such a sinner as I am. It seems
she sets up for a saint.''

"Fred,'' his father said, "none of that,
my boy. No such comments on Margaret.
It may be she knows what she is about better than I do. When her mother joined the
church, I was about your age. I felt then
as if I should like to do the same myself.
But I have hardly thought about it since I
came here to live. But we won't hurt her
feelings, at all events.''

Fred made no reply, but took his hat and
sauntered off. He reached the church just
as the minister parted from Mag at the door.
They appeared to have been talking together,
for several people were waiting a little apart
for Dr. Harris. Fred looked at Margaret
with some curiosity. Certainly religion did
not make her unhappy ; and how lovely she
looked. She was close to him before she

noticed him; so close that she almost started as she exclaimed,

"Why, Fred, were you in church?"

"No, I was not; but I suppose I may come to meet the prettiest girl who was there, if I chose."

"O certainly! where is she? let me have a look at her as you join her," replied Mag, feigning ignorance.

"Well, her dinner will be cold if she don't come home; so let us hurry along," said Fred. Mag laughed, and the walk home, Fred had to confess, was not marred by any want of congeniality between them.

In the meantime, Kitty and Laura were pursuing very different trains of thought. Laura was steeling herself against the possibility of an "attack" from Margaret.

"She won't let me alone long now," she thought. "She will feel that she has asserted her superior stand now, and she will seize the opportunity. She shan't, she shan't! I'll quarrel with her first."

Quarrel with Margaret! The idea struck her as preposterous, and forced a smile involuntarily to her face; but her last determination was not to yield one inch.

Kitty was more impressed than she would have liked to own. She had a sort of undefined yearning after the peace which Margaret possessed. And she had been convinced that it needed more than the difference in their natural temperaments to account for it.

"I know I am impulsive, and she is quiet," said she to herself. "But Laura is as quiet as Mag; and yet, there's a difference. Mag is never ruffled; little vexations don't seem to be vexations to her; everything seems to go well with her; and such absolute unselfishness I never saw. How she did listen to that garrulous old Mrs. Jameson, the other night, as if she were the person she most desired to talk with, when she knew perfectly well that Prof. Simms was explaining all about the spectroscope, over which she and Laura have gone wild. I couldn't have done it. I don't suppose I would have been rude, but I should have managed it somehow. I guess I would have turned the old lady over to some one else, if she had known my father when he was a boy. I don't know but what, some day, I'll ask her about it. I don't believe I'd mind it, if she put me in the way of being better than I am now. There's room for improvement, and there's no one I'd rather be like than Mag."

Margaret's account of the day will be best given in her own words, as she jotted it down for Emily's benefit that evening.

" Emily dear,

It is Sabbath evening, and it has been Communion Sabbath here. I thought of you all last Sunday, and should have been so glad if the Communion had occurred here on the same day. But I could hardly have had a happier day than this has been. There was only one thing hard, — to sit all alone in Uncle Henry's pew; to see the whole family leave, — deliberately turn their backs on Christ's table. It almost broke my heart. And I felt as if I could do nothing but pray, pray, pray, for them. It was my first communion away from home. How strange it seemed not to see your father at the table. I missed him sadly at first; but he was right in telling me I should love Dr. Harris. I have been delighted with his sermons from the very first, they are so essentially practical. He always gives one something to carry home, and his illustrations are wonderful. They are nearly always drawn from every-day life, but are applied in a way that must leave an impression, it seems to me. It is so much easier to remember his sermons than most people's; perhaps because they are rendered very personal. He never, no matter what his subject is, neglects an appeal to those who are not Christians, often making it in just a very few words, but in such words that I do not see how they can fail of their mark. It seems impossible, to me, that any one should sit unmoved under his preaching. I have met him several times, and always with great pleasure. And to-day his greeting went to my very heart. I suppose it was because I had never been anywhere but at home, that the invitation to strangers struck me with such peculiar force. "It is not our table, but the Lord's," Dr. Harris said. And it made me feel that Christians are indeed one family everywhere;

and that although lonely, I was not alone.
Coming out, Dr. Harris stopped me for one
moment, and in his fatherly way, " Good-
morning, dear,'' he said. " I was very glad
to see that you were with us in the service
of the Master." I thanked him, and he
said : " It is the Lord who has brought you
among us, and he will give you work to do,
no doubt, my dear. You may do a very
great work in your uncle's family.'' I could
not speak; my heart was full. His words
were sweet to me, but yet they frightened
me. O Emily, I do so long to tell the girls
something of Christ ! It is so sad to see them
living without Him. And yet I don't know
how. The responsibility overpowers me.
Laura, I am sure, would never bear a single
word. Kitty might just tolerate it, because
she is the personification of good-nature.
But even she, I think, in her heart, would
resent the attempt. I am afraid to speak

once, lest it should estrange them and prevent any further intimacy. The boys, too,
trouble me. Fred, I can see, thinks religion is old women's talk. Aunt Alice herself told me that he prides himself upon being
a man of the world. He is extremely popular, even courted, and exposed to all the
temptations which surround an attractive
young man with plenty of money, in this
city. Frank is much more quiet in his tastes
than Fred, and engrossed, most of the time,
with his books. He is younger, and does
not care yet to go much into society, though
he enjoys the friends who come to the house
here as much, in his own way, as Fred does.
I am very fond of Frank, indeed. I hardly
know which of the two I love best. Fred
came to church to meet me to-day. They
are both as good as they can be to me. Art
is a fine boy, and Sue is a darling. I wrote
you that I was teaching her. I enjoy it very

much, and yet I feel like a coward when I look at her. I am really afraid to talk to her as I would like, lest she should repeat it all, and I should not only be laughed at, but should lose all chance of reaching Laura and the boys. You see, dear, how weak I am, and how helpless. Yet I think I could speak if I were sure I ought; sure that it would not do more harm than good. You must help me with all your might in your prayers and in your letters. And pray for all of them here, won't you? I cannot be faithless; I must hope that the time may come when I shall see them all brought into the safe fold.

There is a large mission school connected with the church here. I went into it one day with Uncle Henry, who contributes largely to its support, and it interested me exceedingly. You can scarcely imagine any two schools more unlike than that and our quiet little country school. They have, here, all the modern contrivances and machinery of which you and I have read, rather wonderingly, in the Sunday School Times. The superintendent gave a lesson on the blackboard while I was there, a very good one. I think it is a great accessory to any school, and I don't see why we should not introduce one into ours. Suppose you bring up the subject at the next teachers' meeting. I have been thinking of taking a class in the mission. I know I should enjoy it, and I might, perhaps, do some good in that way. I have not spoken of it here, but I do not believe Uncle Henry would have any objection to it, even if he only looked upon it as a whim of mine. He is most anxious that I should gratify my own tastes and inclinations in every thing; and if he sees that I really desire to do this, I am sure he will not say no. If I do go into it you may

expect to hear full accounts of all the proceedings, and I shall depend upon you to
report particulars to Miss Harriet and Miss
Chryssie, — you remember their talk about
such things when I went to bid them good-
bye. I am glad to hear that Aunt Dinah is
so well this winter. Tell her I met an old
auntie in the street, the other day, who reminded me of her. And Uncle Henry's
servants are all colored people. The cook
was formerly a slave, though she was not
one who ran away to seek her liberty. She
was set free by the provisions of her master's will. It is bed-time now, so I must
say good-night. Write very soon to

Your loving MARGARET.

CHAPTER XII.

In the course of the week following the Communion Sabbath, Dr. Harris dined at Mr. Chauncey's, and during the evening he took occasion to say to Margaret,

"How would you like to help us in our Mission School, Miss Margaret?"

Margaret told him that she had been thinking of it for a week or two. That she had had a class at home, and had missed it sorely. But that she had hesitated somewhat, partly because her stay was not to extend beyond the spring, partly because she did not know many of those engaged in the school, and partly from a distrust of her own powers; it seemed such a different matter to take charge of those wild street-children, from teaching her own class of the children of her friends at home.

" Have you visited the school at all? " asked Dr. Harris.

Yes, Margaret said she had, and had thought it presented a very interesting field of labor. She had never seen so many children together, nor any assemblage of children of that stamp, and she had been very much struck with some of the faces.

" And I know you are fond of children, from the way little Susie has found her way to your heart? "

" O yes, I am; though I do not think any one could resist Sue's charms."

" Did you see my daughter the day you visited the school? "

12

" No, sir; I did not know she was there. It is strange I did not recognize her."

" She is in a separate room. She has a large class of half-grown girls, dressmakers' apprentices, bonnet-frame makers, girls in stores, &c., &c., all of them dependent on their own exertions, some of them obliged to be the main stay of their families. She has some very interesting cases among them, and she is heart and soul in the work. Her labors have been blessed, too. Two of the girls were among those who united with the church yesterday; and I think others will follow. I hope you will decide to help us. We need teachers very much. It is just as it always has been, — ' The harvest is great and the laborers are few.' Think the matter over, and if you conclude to take a class, Ellen will be delighted to call for you, next Sabbath, and introduce you. Or if you have not then decided, suppose you go with her once, at any rate, and see if the deeper insight into the work will not persuade you."

" I do not think I need persuasion, sir, if you think I am able to undertake it. Though, of course, I cannot promise without consulting my uncle. He may have some objections."

" I do not think he will. And as to capability, I should mistrust any one likely to go in her own strength. But I should not be afraid of the weakest who undertakes in the name of the Strength-giver. I shall expect to hear of your enrolment next Sabbath, then.''

After Dr. Harris had gone, Margaret informed her uncle that he had asked her to take a class, and that she was inclined to undertake it, but had told him that she could not promise before speaking to her uncle.

" Do you really want to do it," asked her

uncle, "or is it a piece of self-denial for Dr. Harris's or conscience' sake?"

"Why, I really want to, sir. I always have taught at home. And then, I do think I am leading a very idle sort of life here."

"German, music, singing lessons, teaching Sue, to say nothing of incidentals," ejaculated Fred. "A new definition of idleness.'"

"But none of these can be called work, Fred. They are far too pleasant to be classed under that head; and besides, they are purely self-indulgent. But Uncle, why did you ask?"

"Because, my dear, I think teaching in a Mission School is very laborious, and involves much self-denial. Dr. Harris is very persuasive, and a certain young lady is very easily made to believe that a disagreeable undertaking is a duty. I don't want you to be imposed upon; but if you really want

to try your hand upon some of the city
Arabs, it makes no kind of difference to
me."

"But Mag," remonstrated Laura, "I
don't believe you know what you are about,
indeed I don't. Your class at home was
something very different, I should think.
These children are brought in from such
dreadful places. I went to the anniversary
once, and heard the reports of the Bible
readers, I believe they call them. It was
dreadful. I made up my mind then, that
the whole work was a mystery to me. And
then they are so dirty,— ugh! it makes me
shudder to think of them. The atmosphere
of that room was awful, even on Anniversary
Day. And when I said so to Ellen Harris
she laughed at me, and said it was pure
country air, compared with what it sometimes was. Nonsense, Marge! It is such
exhausting work. You have no idea of it.

Ellen looks utterly fagged out on Sunday afternoons; and she is considered a strong girl, you know. You had better not try it, indeed, Margery."

" Besides,'' said Fred, " you don't even have the satisfaction of accomplishing anything, that I can see. Charley Jones had a class for six months, and he said a more thankless task he never undertook. The boys played every prank upon him that ever was heard of ; treated him abominably ; tore up the Testaments he gave them, and actually asked him for money for all sorts of things. He left in disgust."

" As to that," said Laura, who was noted for her justice to every one, " I doubt whether Charley's teaching would interest any one, to begin with ; or whether he tried very hard to do his duty there. Every one knows that he went there, not to teach his boys, but to walk home with a certain one of the teachers; and I imagine the walking home was the only part he found suited to his taste. But the dirt is the most dreadful part to me. And then the possibility of infection. O Mag, suppose you should contract some disease!"

"If she should," said Aunt Alice, "I don't doubt we should all try to take care of her. But I don't believe she will. I don't believe the risks that are run are very great, for see how many do teach in them, and visit the children in their homes; and I never knew a person who contracted disease. I say, try it, Margie. If it proves too much for you, you must give it up, that's all."

"Thank you, very much, Auntie. It is real good to have some one on my side against the attacks of Fred and the girls. They have drawn a doleful picture of the work. But it has occurred to me, perhaps they do not see as much of it as would warrant the delineation, after all."

She said it a little mischievously, and Kitty and Fred laughed; but Laura drew herself up a little stately. It seemed to her like a loop-hole, and she was determined that no reproaches should creep in.

"I have seen quite as much of it as I desire," she said severely.

Poor Laura! she was showing her worst side. She was so attractive; in so many ways a noble girl. But the fear that some one would suggest to her, what in her heart of hearts she knew to be her duty, made her assume this repellant, defiant air when any point was touched which could, in any way, lead to the subject of personal religion.

The others saw how she felt, and hastened to change the subject. Nothing more was said of the school till just as Margaret was going to bed, when Mr. Chauncey called her back.

" Then you think you will take a class next Sunday, Mag?"

" Yes, sir; I had better begin at once."

" Very well, dear. As you please. How much you look like your mother, Margaret. There, good-night, and God bless you, Mag."

" He never said that to me before," thought Margaret, as she went up stairs. " O God bless him! "

" She is a dear child," was his reflection, " and I do believe a true Christian. There are true Christian women, I suppose. I cannot doubt it when I remember my own mother, and see Mag's mother, and Mag herself. But men are so different."

So he stifled conscience, as do so many, alas! looking at human imperfection, instead of to the Great Example; picking the mote out of their brother's eye, when behold, a beam is in their own eye.

CHAPTER XIII.

That same week brought the necessity for deciding upon one of those questions which Margaret had anticipated, but which she had not yet answered. The really gay season was but just beginning in New York. The entertainments to which our young people had, so far, been invited, were of rather a quiet, social order. There had been some dancing, but it had not been the exclusive occupation of the evening. Margaret had given the matter a great deal of thought. And in her own mind she had become more

than convinced in her first impression, that
between the square dances and the round
there was a vast difference; almost so great
as to exclude all possibility of regarding
them as on a footing.

"I am sure," she wrote to her mother,
"I cannot conceive of any harm coming
from a moderate indulgence in the square
dances. I am sure that if some one introduced the Lancers among some of our unso-
phisticated friends at Rowenah, and called it
a game and not a dance, even Deacon Wood
would look upon it with a friendly eye, and
no more dream of harm ensuing than from
a Thanksgiving game of Blind Man's Buff
in his great kitchen, at home. The round
dances are different. I can see the fasci-
nation in them, to a certain extent; and I
have danced several times with Fred, at
home, when there was no company. He
says I learn quickly. I suppose my ear for

music helps me. But the idea of dancing so with a stranger, or even with a friend, is revolting to me. The square dances I shall enjoy in company, and I think I have decided rightly. The round dances I would willingly engage in, with our own boys, but with no one else. And as, of course, I cannot make this discrimination at parties, I shall limit my indulgence in them to Uncle Henry's own house, and that, when there are no visitors present. I have not said anything about this since I first plead ignorance; and Fred probably thinks I have yielded, or lost my verdancy, as he would probably term it. Of course, when the occasion comes, I must take my stand. And I hope, in the meantime, to hear from you and Papa that you approve of my position. You left it entirely to myself, so that I have stated it as a decision. Of course it is subject to your criticism. You all know that I

have not come to it alone. And I think I
have been led to decide as I would wish
to see Walter and Rob do. As to the other
amusements, I am still at sea. It is doing
me good to think so much about these
things, I know. And I am trusting that
strength will be given equal to my day."

The occasion upon which Margaret felt that
the battle must be fought and won with her
cousins came one morning at the breakfast-
table, when invitation-cards were brought
in addressed to all the young people, in-
cluding Margaret.

Mrs. Turner's, Friday night, of next week.

" O delightful ! " exclaimed Kitty. " Her
parties are always so charming."

And " delightful " was echoed by Laura
and Fred, while even stay-at-home Frank
conceded that this promised better than most
such invitations.

" Get your dancing-boots, Marge," said

Fred, "and we will have a private rehearsal every night. I can teach you the German in less time than that."

"Thank you, Fred, but I think this," — holding up Ahn, which she had been studying before breakfast, — "will be all the German I shall care to master."

"Nonsense!" Fred retorted. "No bashfulness or modesty either. You shall be my partner first, and I can promise to carry any girl safely through any dance."

"I really cannot, Fred. You mustn't ask me. I will dance with you at home, and I'll dance the square dances with your friends; but indeed you must not ask me to dance the round dances with strangers; and of course, if I am seen dancing with you, I must dance with any who may ask."

"Sancta Margherita!" There was a sneer in Fred's voice, though he meant it to pass for a jest. It hurt Mag, and so did Laura's elevated eye-brows. Kitty and Frank listened intently. Mr. Chauncey was hidden behind his newspaper.

" I am not a ' saint,' Fred, and I am very sorry that our opinions clash on any point. I love to meet your friends, and to go out with you ; and I am very much obliged to you for caring, as you do, to have me go. There are not many things that any of you could ask which I could decline doing. But there are some in which you must let me take my own stand. I do it at the risk of being called stubborn, or odd, which is the greater crime of the two in the eyes of this world of ours, is it not?" she added, forcing a laugh.

" Margaret," — her uncle had taken up the thread, — " my child, is this decision based on your own principles or on your parents' wishes ? "

" It is my own doing, sir. Papa and

Mamma left all these questions entirely with me. It would have been much easier to have a command from them, but they would not give me one.''

Her voice trembled. The effort was very great, but she had to go on.

" Uncle Henry, you know what I profess to be. I have tried to decide from that standpoint in this matter."

" Then you condemn all the amusements concerning which so much has been said and written of late days? "

" No, Uncle Henry ; on some of them, my mind is completely in the dark, as yet. I have lived so quietly in the country that I have never had occasion to give special attention to these questions; but I know they must all be solved this winter. And I hope you all understand,'' she said emphatically, and with an uneasy glance at Laura and Fred, " that I only decide for myself. It seems to me impossible for any one to lay down general principles with regard to these amusements. I think the principles lie far back of them. And I do not dream of condemning those who decide in opposition to my opinions. I only ask the same toleration from others, Fred,'' she said, holding out her hand.

"It's a free country,'' said Fred, taking it, "so I must grant a truce. I can't help being disappointed, and I never expect to be convinced that you are right. But I won't persecute you. You are honest, at all events; and I know that if you change your opinions you'll say so. My offer for a waltz holds good permanently. When you are ready to take it, say so.'' And he went off.

"She's a trump, anyhow," he said. "I like the stuff she's made of, but it's been spoiled in the fashioning. It's prejudice, every bit of it. There can't be any harm in it. There are men, of course, one don't care to see one's sisters dancing with, but it doesn't do them any real harm."

Margaret left the table just after Fred, in order to add a postscript to a letter she wished to despatch early.

After she had gone, " That girl has got grit in her," said Frank.

" She's a noble girl," said his father. " I wish there were a few more like her in firmness of character, though I do not agree with her on this point. Laura, you look disturbed."

" Papa, I don't want to be cross, and I do admire Margaret's boldness; but I wish she did not think so. It is very unpleasant. There will be conflicts all winter. I would so much rather have her go heart and soul with us in everything. The Mission School disturbed me first, and now this has come right on top of it. She will be loving those horrible little mission children, or her work among them, so much, that she will prefer them to our friends. Besides," she added, with a little pardonable consciousness, " it will be very unnatural, Papa, for one of our set to be a wall-flower."

Kitty laughed outright. " Margaret a wall-flower! My dear Laura, where have your eyes been at the little companies that have been given, so far. I am sure you need not distress yourself on that point. She will dance the square dances, and as to the rest, I will tell you what I think. If I had Mag's powers of conversation I think I could afford not to dance. And I think, as the summing up of the whole matter, I think that Mag's a darling."

Mag's entrance with her finished letter made this a conclusion indeed.

" Aunt Alice," she said, handing her letter to her uncle to post, " or rather, Laura,

I want to claim your help. I have no finery suitable for the grand affair this party promises to be, and I promised Mamma I would wear white to the first large party we attended. Can you help me choose it to-day? "

There was tact in Margaret's choice of a companion. Laura was born to be a leader, and she liked to be consulted.

" You do care something for the vanities of this world, then," she said. " I needn't give you up altogether, then? "

" I care very much to be prettily dressed," said Mag, " if that is what you are aiming at. Just as prettily and as becomingly as possible. Just as handsomely as my means will allow. I don't think a woman has any right to neglect dress. I would almost say one extreme was as bad as the other.''

"I'm so glad," said Laura. "But this time, Mamma, I won't tell your secret.

"Your dress is up stairs, Margie," Aunt Alice said, smiling. "I foresaw this or a similar emergency, and Laura and you can, at any time, be fitted for each other. White it is. You will not object to a trimming of green, will you?"

"Why, it's the very trimming I had on my mind," cried Margaret. "Aunt Alice, you will smother me with love." And she kissed her aunt two or three times.

"Now run and try it on, and let me see how it looks, dear."

And the two girls darted off as merrily and blithely as if one of them had not just manifested a degree of heroism which, at other times, and under different circumstances, might have sent her to the stake.

The party was a brilliant success. Margaret enjoyed herself thoroughly, as did all the guests, apparently. Once in the course of the evening, as she was talking in her most animated manner to a gentleman whose acquaintance she had just made, Fred stopped at her side for one moment.

" Ready for a galop now, Margery?" he asked, with a mischievous emphasis on the now.

Mag shook her head.

" Do not let me detain you," said Mr. Montgomery. " I can finish my story when you are resting after your dance."

" O no, indeed! thank you. I do not dance the round dances, and my cousin knows it. He is only teasing me a little."

Fred passed on, and Mr. Montgomery replied :

" I have found the eighth wonder. A young lady in New York, in this year of our Lord, daring to confess that she does not dance the round dances. I should not have been so bold at your age, though now that my dancing days are over I can see the evils resulting from the practice."

When they reached home, that night, Kitty went into her father's library where he was awaiting them. Laura followed. Mag was still in the hall, talking over some of the events of the evening with Fred.

" Papa," said Kitty, " I wish you had been with us to see Margaret. She was fairly radiant; and she won admiration from every one. Mr. Montgomery talked to her for a long while, and afterwards spoke of her to Mrs. Turner in the most exalted terms, praising her appearance, her intellect, and especially her conversational powers. She charmed Dr. Herz, the Norwegian whom you met the other day, by talking French with him, and you know she has not ventured upon that before in public. In short, the evening was a grand success for her."

"And yet, Laura, she didn't dance the round dances."

"No, Papa. I was very foolish this morning to say that about a wall-flower. There are girls whose feet are the only educated part of them, and I know how it would be if they did not dance. I never should have compared Mag to them."

"And since it is a matter of principle with Margaret, I am sure, Laura, you would be the last one to have her yield for the sake of a little fleeting enjoyment, or even to win admiration. I am sure she deserves more praise for her adherence to her principles than Ferrero's aptest pupil ever merited."

"Of course she does, Papa, and I honor her for it, though the wish that our opinions did not clash still remains."

"Well, Laura," said Kitty, "better get rid of the wish, for you will never bring Mag round to your way of thinking."

"And I will never go round to hers, you think, Kit? Well, I don't think I ever shall; at least, not till my dancing days are over. Good-night, Papa."

"Good-night, my darlings. It is high time to go to bed. Fred, you'll be sleepy over the books to-morrow. Country lassie, I will not have the roses driven out of your cheeks by late hours. I am glad you enjoyed the evening so well. Good-night, all of you."

CHAPTER XIV.

True to an appointment made after her
conversation with Dr. Harris, Margaret was
ready early on the morning of the following
Sabbath when Miss Harris called for her.
Fred had greeted her as Ma'am Missionary,
when he appeared just as she was leaving
the table, but no other remarks had been
made. Her own mind was full of many
thoughts. She dreaded, on some accounts,
the attempt she was about to make, for she
knew the work must be arduous. But at
the same time she was looking forward

eagerly to her untried field. The very novelty of it made it interesting, and she wondered what sort of children would be put
under her care ; asking herself, over and over
again, whether she would be able to subdue
them if they should belong to the ungovern-
able tribes of which he had sometimes read.

"I am so glad you are ready in good
season," said Miss Harris, as they left the
house. "We have a prayer-meeting of the
teachers for a few minutes before school,
and I find it the greatest help to me. Every
one seems so earnest there. It is drawing
the last buckle in our armor, and I feel as
if I were not wholly equipped if I am too
late for it."

"I am glad to know of it, and I hope I
shall always be able to attend. Uncle Henry
likes breakfast tolerably early, and I do not
anticipate any difficulty. Fortunately, I have
not very far to go. But I want you to tell

me something about the order of exercises in your school. I was not present at the opening, the day I was there."

Her request was, of course, complied with. And the description occupied most of the time consumed in the walk, until, just before reaching the chapel, Miss Harris asked Margaret,

" Have you any preference as to your class? Do you want girls or boys? "

" O," Margaret said, " the idea of boys never entered my mind. I supposed girls would be given me, of course."

" I asked you because there is a class of boys, which young Mr. Jones had for a few months, which is sadly in need of a teacher; and I know Mr. Locke is very anxious to provide for them. They are pretty wild, and perhaps it would be too much for you."

" Mr. Jones! Is that Fred's friend, Charley Jones? "

" Yes. Have you met him? "

" No ; but Fred was speaking of the class the other evening, and quoting Mr. Jones's experience by way of dissuading me from undertaking the work."

"Well," said Miss Harris, " I don't know much about Mr. Jones, and perhaps I ought not to condemn him, especially as I am not in the room at all.   But from what I have heard, I fancy there was a good deal to be said on both sides of that question. The boys are a wild set, it is impossible to deny. But I rather doubt if Mr. Jones was equal to the emergency of controlling them. I know, for one thing, he was not one of the punctual ones ; and I almost feel as if a teacher who habitually allows himself to be late, might as well stay away. Five minutes will demoralize a class of those boys left to themselves. I have seen it, often. Then, when the boys were unruly Mr. Jones

sometimes lost his temper and sometimes
laughed. It is hard enough to restrain one's
risibilities sometimes, I confess; for these
children are wonderfully smart. But of
course it does not tend to improve them if
one does laugh at them. Then, — ''

" But indeed, Miss Harris, I shall not dare
undertake such a class as that. I know nothing, whatever, of such 'emergencies,' as
you may well call them."

" O well, of course I have nothing to
say. Here comes Mr. Locke, however, and
he will have something to urge about that
very class, if I am not mistaken; for I
know its want of a teacher lies very near
his heart.''

" Mr. Locke, I am so happy as to bring
a recruit this morning. Miss Worthington
is spending the winter at Mr. Chauncey's,
and has undertaken to help us here."

" I am very glad, indeed. I assure you

we need teachers very much. Will you sit with Miss Harris till school is opened? for it is almost time for prayer-meeting now; and as soon as class-teaching begins, I will come for you."

They passed into a pleasant little room.

"This is my sanctum," said Miss Harris. "But my girls are with the whole school, at the opening, and so we have our meeting here."

There were about fifteen already assembled, and Mr. Locke at once began:

"God has given each of us, to-day, one more opportunity of reaching out, to starving creatures, the bread of life. If they only knew that they were starving, half the work would be accomplished. But alas! they say, 'I am rich and increased in goods, and have need of nothing.' May we go to them as we have never gone before, and as if we never expected to go again. And may the Spirit fill our hearts and theirs. Let us pray."

A very few words followed, but they were earnest, pleading words. Then a verse of a hymn was sung; then another short prayer made. Then one of the gentlemen made a single practical remark about what he called the key-note of the lesson they were to teach that morning. And then a few moments were devoted to silent prayer. And then the superintendent, by rising, gave the signal for adjourning to the main room. And as Margaret saw the solemn and intent look upon the faces of the teachers, she did not wonder that Miss Harris had called their little morning meeting one of her greatest helps.

She sat with Miss Harris at one side of the superintendent's desk, where she could see nearly all the scholars, and a wonderful sight it was that greeted her eyes. Four hundred faces up-turned towards Mr. Locke. Four hundred, and no two alike. Some there were with the round, rosy faces which children ought to wear. But alas! how few and far between they were. They gave tokens of a mother's care, and of a home from whose doors the wolf had some how or other been kept away. But how many, O how many, were thin and wan and poorly-clad. How many looked as if a wholesome meal was something they had never known. Nor were these the ones which sent the saddest thrill through Margaret's heart. For there were some whose faces showed a hardness of expression which nothing but long familiarity with unkind treatment, or with neglect, or with crime, ever gives. There were girls whose faces bore deep lines of care. There were boys on whom sin had stamped lines of shrewdness and craftiness and passion, pitiful to behold upon those who were scarcely beyond the days of childhood. Margaret's heart shrank from the possibility of coming into contact with any of these; and yet she yearned for power to smooth one brow. She looked about her, in search of a class which might answer to the descriptions she had heard of Mr. Jones's, and soon detected t. Five boys, from twelve to fourteen years of age, without a teacher; restless to the last degree. It did not seem to her that they were quiet for a single instant. The general order of the school was excellent, and the superintendent's eye was too often cast over towards their corner to allow of any very noisy outbreak. And yet Margaret noticed that even his vigilant supervision did not hinder them from some disorderly pranks. They joined in the singing most lustily. In fact, each one appeared to be vieing with the other in the effort to make a noise. And as the hymn was sung to one of the liveliest of Sunday School tunes, the effect was overpowering, and appeared to cause the boys a great deal of amusement. The opening of the Bibles in the next room was the occasion of animated whispering among them. And glances and even touches of warning and reproof from neighboring teachers were entirely and openly disregarded whenever Mr. Locke appeared to be observing the other side of the school. While the sudden look of propriety and devotion which was assumed when his eyes turned towards their class, seemed to Margaret a wonderful piece of acting. She did not, of course, watch them during prayer-time; but she could not fail to perceive that their opportunity for carrying out their own plans would reach its climax then. " Who is sufficient for these things? " she asked. And her own strength seemed as absolutely nothing. But in spite of their behavior these boys had already interested her, and she recalled the promise, "My strength is made perfect in weakness,'' and was by no means so averse to trying them as she had been when Miss Harris had first mentioned the matter. After all that had been said, she was prepared to have Mr. Locke urge this class upon her. He came, as he had promised, just as Miss Harris was passing into the class-room, and sat down by her. After a few questions about her home, her former class, &c., he said:

"Now, Miss Worthington, I wonder if I may venture to put you in the thickest of the fight at once?" And he repeated what she had already heard of the class.

"But, Mr. Locke, is it customary to give such a class to a lady?"

"It is not unusual. And I am particularly anxious that the experiment should be tried in this case. The class has been neg-

lected.   I am afraid its last teacher failed
to do the boys justice, and it is already
some weeks since he left.   I have tried in
vain to find a successor; and I was just about
on the point of dividing them among two or
three classes.   This I did not at all want
to do.   They have been together for some
time, and I have felt anxious that they should
go on as they have begun.   I think there
are some ways in which a lady is eminently
qualified to be successful in this particular
sphere.   Kindness, provided it be joined to
firmness, invariably, I believe, tells on these
boys sooner or later.   And a lady can appeal to the chivalry which exists somewhere
in every boy's heart, whereas that is a shaft
which a gentleman does not possess.   Besides, Miss Worthington, those boys are not
altogether bad.   They are fun-loving, mis-
chief-making boys, and they are exposed to
temptations which you and I can hardly

conceive. But I believe there is much good in them all, though it is hidden away beneath a vast amount of rubbish. They have been greatly demoralized lately, for they have been at the mercy of any stray teacher who has happened to be with us. I think it does them very great credit that they have been here regularly. A great many would have gone off in this interim. They feel the want of a teacher, too. One or two of them have come to me and said, 'Mr. Locke, ain't you going to get a teacher for us?' Perhaps this will tend to dispose them favorably to any one who is likely to be regular. What do you say?"

"I hardly know what to say. My heart has warmed towards them as you have spoken, and yet I am so afraid of making a failure of the attempt."

"Well, will you take them this morning? That will give you an opportunity to judge

further of the work. And if, at the end of
the session, you are afraid to commit yourself, I will provide a less trying class for
you."

"That I should like to do, very much."

And as it was already late, Mr. Locke led
her at once to the seat.

" Boys, this lady is going to take care of
you to-day. And if you are very good,
perhaps she will take your class for the
winter. It depends on your behavior this
morning. Can I trust you not to drive her
away from you? "

" Yes, sir," answered one or two. But
one, the largest one, said, as Mr. Locke left
them,

" I don't want no lady teacher. I'm going out."

" Stop one moment," Margaret said, as
he attempted to pass her. " That is not
being quite fair, is it? We are to try each

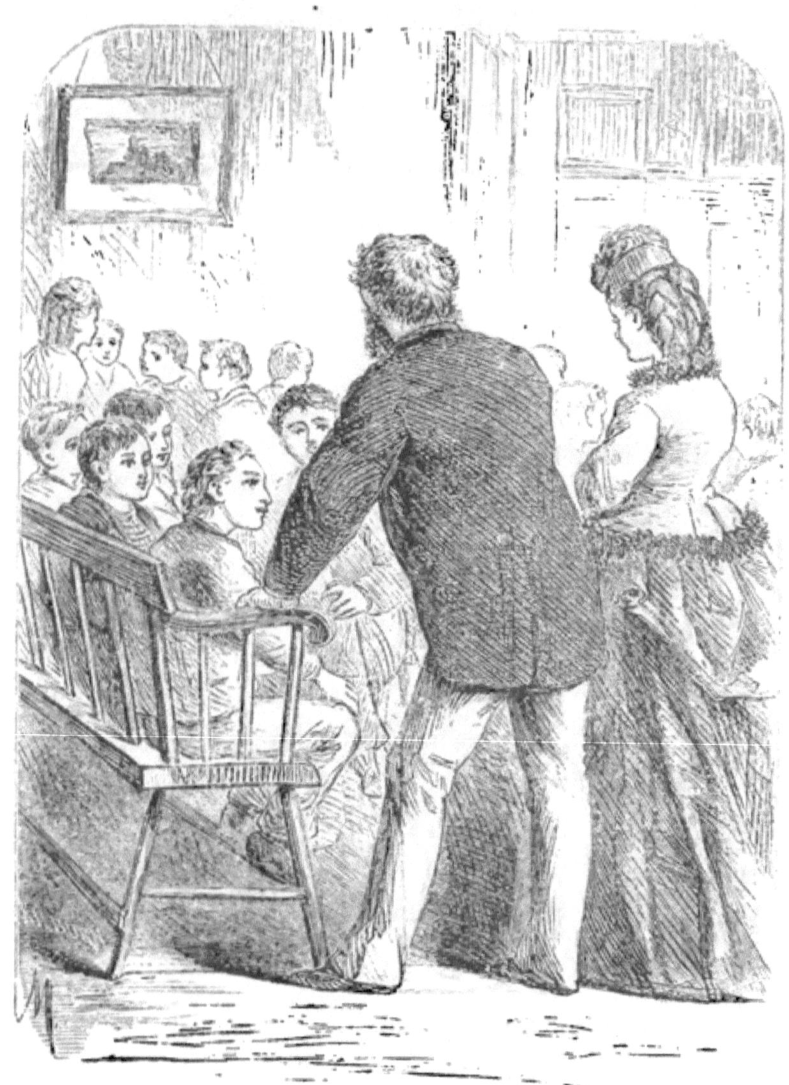

Boys, this lady is going to take care of you to-day.   Page 216.

other this morning, and if I like the class, and all but you like me for their teacher, I promise to ask Mr. Locke to put you in some gentleman's class. Is not that a fair bargain?"

There's a wonderful charm in the word "fair," to most boys. It has worked marvels in more than one Sabbath School class. And the boy sat down, a little bit ashamed of himself.

"Now, boys, we must get acquainted with each other. My name is Miss Worthington, and yours?" She paused, but no one ventured to take the lead. She was obliged to appeal to each one in turn.

"John Schopp, Fred Dulzheimer, Andrew Schmidt, Tom McKay, and Charley Schaeffer,'' she read from the list she had made, as they had spoken.

"Were you all born in New York?" she said.

"No, ma'am.   I came from Germany," said Fred.

" And I, — and I," exclaimed John and Andrew.

" I didn't, but my mother and father did," said Charley.

" My mother is Scotch," vouchsafed little Tom.   " Father was Scotch, too, but he's dead."

" Is he?   Then who takes care of you? "

" O, Mother.   She takes in washing, and I peddles matches and lead pencils.   I makes twelve shillin' a week some times."

" And do you all work for your living? "

" Of course.   What else could we do? " asked Fred.

" You might go to school, you know."

" Father has too many children to keep me at school,'' was Fred's reply.   " I'm learning the printer's trade."

" Well, if I am your teacher, I hope I

shall know all about your families soon. But now we must see about the lesson. Have you your Testaments or Bibles here? "

" There's two old Bibles in the drawer," and Andrew produced them.

" And did you have any verses to learn at home? "

There was no answer.

" Don't you learn verses out of the Bible? ' '

" Ain't got no Bible," said Charley.

" No Bible, Charley? "

" No; Mother's got a German one, but no one ever reads it, that I see."

" Have you no Bible either, Fred? ' '

" Yes; but I don't learn no lessons.''

" Why not, Fred? "

" Don't want to," was the frank reply.

" But, Fred, what if every one only did what they wanted to. Suppose Mother didn't want to mend your clothes or cook your dinner, how would you feel? "

He was a little staggered at being treated in a reasonable manner. And she turned to Andrew just as a pellet of tin foil, aimed by Charley, reached his cheek, and produced a loud " Ow " from Andrew, and a smothered cachinnation from the rest of the class. Margaret was aghast! She had never dreamed of such proceedings. And when she turned around and saw Fred displaying the rubber head of a man capable of any amount of horrible distortions of countenance to poor little well-meaning Tommy McKay, her amazement reached its climax. She looked nervously at the clock, and saw that church time was approaching; and feeling that she must summon all her faculties to make a bold stand, she exclaimed:

" Boys, I want every one of you to listen to me, without attending to anything else, until Mr. Locke rings his bell. New York boys think that they know a great deal; and they are apt to laugh at any one who comes from the country. Now I am from the country, and I have taught in Sunday School there. And I must tell you I never saw any children behave as you have done to-day. I do not see any reason why you and I should not be real good friends; but we must understand each other at the outset. I promise to do my part of the work as well as I can, and I expect you to do the same. As well as you can,— no better. But you will find, perhaps, that I think you are able to do better than you ever have done before. Try for next Sunday. And now just one word more. You all know that Jesus Christ came to save you from your sins. And yet you are going on in your sins. I want you to ask yourselves, before next Sunday, whether, when he has done so much for you, it is not time for you to begin to do something for Him? And then I will try to tell you some of the things you can do.'"

The bell rang, and after some general exercises, school was dismissed. Little Tommy lingered behind the others, and said:

"Teacher, I learned my verses for to-day."

And she heard him recite them even then.

"Teacher, are you going to try our class again? There's some awful bad boys in it, — but we hain't had a teacher for so long!"

She looked down into his face, and said:

"Yes, Tommy, I think I'll try it again."

And Mr. Locke came behind them just in time to hear the promise.

"Well, Miss Worthington, how did it go?"

And Margaret gave him an account of her proceedings.

"I had no time to hear them say any lesson, sir. I do hope though, that next Sunday I shall manage better. I don't want them to begin by managing me."

"I think you will succeed. Here, by the way, is our lesson-paper. In the afternoon, the instruction is all from the desk. But I hope you will be with us."

"O yes, indeed."

"And now, Miss Worthington, I must ask one more bit of information from you. Will you tell me when your birthday occurs?"

Margaret did not know whether she had heard aright, but she answered at once,

"The 18th of April, sir."

He made a note of it, and drew a card from his pocket.

"Here is a list of our teachers, with the

date of each one's birthday.   Last Christmas we instituted the practice of remembering each birthday as a season of prayer for that teacher.   And although some greeted the little card with a smile at first, I really think we have all found it a bond of union to one another."

She thanked him for the card, and went to church.

Laura and Kitty met her at the door, but there was no time for reporting the morning's proceedings, and no questions were asked of her until the family assembled at dinner.

"Well, Mag," said Aunt Alice, then, "what about Sunday School?"

"O, I became very much interested indeed, Auntie dear.   I think Mr. Locke controls the children admirably."

"And did they find a niche for you?" asked her uncle.

"Yes, indeed; a niche that I am rather afraid to undertake to fill."

" Girls' class or boys'? " asked Frank, laconically.

" Boys' class, Frank. The same one that Mr. Jones taught."

Fred had not meant to engage in the conversation at all; but to listen, and make his own comments. But this announcement took him by surprise, and he broke forth :

" Charley Jones's class ! that set of ragamuffins and villains !   It's the greatest imposition I ever heard of; and Mr. Locke ought to be ashamed of himself. I'll go directly after dinner, — "

" My dear cousin," — and Margaret was laughing at Fred's vehemence, " do listen for one moment. Mr. Locke merely asked me to take the class; and I took it with my eyes wide open. If I cannot manage those boys I will give it up in a very little

15

while. There is no compulsion in the matter."

" But, Mag, I'm almost afraid for your
life. They're a regular set of roughs."

" O no, Fred, I guess not. They are
full of fun and of mischief. But I imagine
there is more good in them than meets the
eye at first. That Fred Dulzheimer seems
to be the leader, and I mean to make friends
with him first, and see if he don't influence
the others."

" Were they very dirty?" asked Laura.

" They were not clean, dear; but yet not
filthy. I did not touch their hands, but they
looked like the hands of hard-working men.
They all work for their living, — those children. It seems cruelty to them that their
parents allow it; and yet, I suppose Fred
Dulzheimer told the whole story when he
said, ' Father's got too many children to
keep me at school.' "

" Yes," said Mr. Chauncey; " it is often just the money that those children bring in that stands between the family and starvation."

" It is terrible, Uncle Henry; and it is dreadful to see the look of care on some of the children, especially the girls. They look like little old women. And some of the boys look so wicked, so used to all sorts of deceit and cunning. I imagine I shall see some phases of the depravity of human nature heretofore unknown to me, before I learn to know my boys very well."

" Did they pay any attention to what you said?" asked Kitty.

" I cannot say that they did. I had a very short time to do anything, it seemed to me. Mr. Locke talked to me for some time before I went to the class; and then he rang the bell very early, because he had some special remarks to make."

" And yet even that time tired you out,'' said Laura. " You looked as if you had done a hard day's work when you came into church. I think it is too much for you."

" I was probably more tired than I ever will be again. Of course there was a good deal of excitement about it, and I confess that I felt utterly lost with regard to managing the boys. So I had a consciousness of not accomplishing anything at all. And it was that which wearied me. I think I shall love the work very much. And I am sure it will be worth all the fatigue if I succeed in helping any of those children in any way."

" I think,'' said Mr. Chauncey, " that the Mission is doing a good work. We need every purifying influence in our city, and our land, that can possibly be introduced. And the effect of the school is civilizing. If it makes useful citizens out of some of those wild street-children, it will not be work thrown away."

Margaret did not reply. But she could not help thinking that while all that her uncle said was most true, it was necessary to make the christianizing of the boys the first matter. If we can only make Christians of them, the desire and ability to be good citizens will follow of necessity, she thought. But if the civilization of them should be undertaken without reference to the change of heart, it would scarcely be possible that the reform would be permanent or life-giving.

"I do wish," said Fred, drawing Mag off into the parlor after dinner, "I do wish you had not gone into the school. There will be no end to the demands made upon your time. I have seen enough of the work to know that."

"Well, Fred, I really think you might

be a little reasonable about it. Is there any one you know of with less tax upon her than I have this winter? I should feel verily guilty if I were not doing something of the kind. See what Miss Harris has to keep her busy besides the school; and yet, how much she accomplishes."

"Well, but Ellen Harris is just made for that kind of thing, you see. She is a real goodish sort of girl, I know; but she has nothing else to recommend her. She is prosy to the last degree, and plain. So it's no wonder she takes up with all that sort of work."

"Really, Fred, I am not sure that your train of reasoning is particularly complimentary to me."

"What do you mean?"

"Why, do you want me to cultivate the ornamental purely, and consider me unfit for anything useful?"

“ Of course not.   But this particular branch of usefulness I think you might have left alone.   To tell the truth, Margery, my heart was set upon seeing you have a good time this winter; and I don’t want to be baffled.’’

“ And you think there is danger that you will be?   O Fred ! ”

“ But really, Mag, I don’t know what to make of you.   Not to dance, and then to pop off into Sunday School just because a parson asks you.”

“ But Fred, do I look or act as if I were not having a good time? ”

“ No; I confess you don’t.”

“ Then you will surely take my word, when my looks substantiate it.   Indeed, indeed, I am having a very good time.   Why, how could I help it?   You are all so good to me, Fred.   You don’t know how it has touched me.   I have said over and over

again, I could not see why you should be.
And I am so glad when there is anything I
can do for you, — you don't know how glad.
And when I do things that displease you,
Fred, it is only because I have one friend
better than any of you here, even. And
my duty to Him must form my chief pleas-
ure. And that's the reason, Fred, why
I must leave you now and go to Sunday
School," she added, rising from the sofa.

He could not help looking after her a little
bit wistfully. " She does have a better time
than most people, I really think," he said.
" But I'll be hanged if I should call Sunday School teaching anything like a good
time."

The afternoon exercises were, as Mr.
Locke told Margaret, entirely from the desk.
But she found that there was plenty to occupy the teachers. The children were even
more restless than in the morning, and much

more dirty. The weekly wash of Saturday night or Sunday morning lost much of its effect during the time between churches. The homes of mission scholars, in a large city, are seldom attractive. And these children were in the habit of spending most of the interval on Sundays in the street, when the weather was at all pleasant,—the very few minutes allotted to their dinner being the only time spent within doors. The consequence was that they came in from all sorts of rough play, the boys at least, and brought with them an amount of animal spirit fearful to cope with. Moreover, they had paid various visits to candy-women and apple-stands, and if the fruit of their purchase had not already disappeared down their throats, it was very apt to be produced from their pockets during the school session. In either case, mouths and fingers bore the traces. The atmosphere, too, was close to the last degree, and gave Margaret a head-ache. And having never been used to just that kind of a Sabbath School, she that afternoon felt keenly all the difficulties under which a teacher labors. She was almost discouraged for a little while; and if Fred had seen the tired and heavy-hearted look upon her face as she left the chapel, he might almost have triumphed. She went into church aching in every bone in her body, and was scarcely conscious of anything that Dr. Harris said; and when she reached home she threw herself on the bed, more exhausted than she had often been in the course of her life. Yet, in spite of this weary feeling, which often almost overcome her on Sabbath afternoons throughout the winter, she learned to see the pleasant side of a teacher's life, and to meet her boys from week to week with real delight.

CHAPTER XV.

Letters between Margaret and her home
had flown with the regularity agreed upon
before her departure from Rowenah. Her
cousins (the girls) complained that she mo-
nopolized the postman's favors; while the
boys offered to advertise in her behalf to
" All persons desiring letters written upon
given subjects,'' and looked with wonder at
the letters she received from her brothers,
declaring that she must have some magic in
her, for they were sure that no one could

extract such epistles from the masculine race
by the use of ordinary means.

One of Walter's letters she one day put
into Fred's hands. And as it had a good
deal of influence upon him, and moreover
awakened in him almost his first real desire
to do good to others, it may be well to give
it here.

" Darling Margery :

I have been missing you
so much lately, there have been so many
things going on in college that really seem
not worth writing about, but yet that I
wanted to talk over with you. But now a
matter has arisen which makes me glad that
you are in New York, because I think you
may gain a hold upon some one who will
surely go down hill very fast if somebody
doesn't lend a helping hand to keep him
back, and turn his footsteps in the right
direction.

Sam Evans has gone one step too far in
his pranks, — just as we have feared he
might do, — and he has been expelled. I
don't blame the Faculty, for they have been
tried to the utmost; and they have been
more patient than could have been expected.
But I am sorry for him, and worried about
him. I dread to think of the possibilities
in his future. You know him, both from
your own experience, and from what I have
told you : how bright he is, and how
popular, and how gentlemanly when with
gentlemen or ladies. You know, too, just
what his stumbling block has been; an in-
ordinate desire for " fun," and an unwillingness to be content with innocent fun.
The lawless pranks attracted him to an as-
tonishing degree, and this trait led him into
company with the boys in college who have
been the means of pushing him on to his
ruin, — that is, as far as college is con-

cerned, — and have managed, by a duplicity of which Sam would scorn to be guilty, to go scot free themselves. The president telegraphed to Sam's uncle, and he came on immediately. Of course he had to, but I almost wish he had stayed away. I don't wonder he is provoked, when Sam is dependent upon him for everything. But he is so very severe that he just hardens Sam. He means well, too. And he is going to send Sam to some wholesale house in New York, in hopes that he will grow steady when he has to work, he says. And here comes the point of my letter: your opportunity and Fred's for doing the boy good. I think his whole life depends now on the influence exerted over him in New York, at the outset. I had a long talk with him last night, and I am more firmly convinced of the correctness of my previous opinion, that he is not an out and out bad fellow. Mind,

I am not justifying his recent behavior,— it has been outrageous. But I think he feels sorry now, and his temptations have been enormous; greater than you can possibly understand. If he falls in with ladies and gentlemen in New York who will be ignorant of, or, at all events will appear ignorant of, his previous history,—who will invite him to their homes, so that he shall not be solely dependent upon low pleasures for entertainment, — if he is attached to some pleasant church, — (I should think, from your letters, that Dr. Harris would be just the pastor for him,) — then, I have great hopes for Sam. If not, if he is left to himself, O Margery! I shudder to think of what may follow. I want you to help along in this affair. I told him, last night, that he must call on you. And he said, rather bitterly : ' A daughter of one of the professors would be so likely to want to see me.'

So you must make some advance, dear. Send him your card, or a note. Or better still, if you can get Fred to call on him, do so. I am very much interested in Sam. And, Margery, there are some of us who have prayed so much for him that we can't give him up while his life lasts. I have filled my whole paper with him, but never mind. He goes down next week. But I don't know yet what his address will be. I will let you have it as soon as I know it myself. Love to all, and especially to Fred, with an entreaty to him to look after poor Sam.

WALTER."

"You will help me in this, won't you, Fred?" asked Margaret.

"I'll do anything I can, Mag; but I don't know how much that will be. I don't understand the business of reforming as well as I do a good many other things."

“ But you’ll call on him?”

“ O yes; and ask him here. But my usual way of looking after strangers committed to my care is to take them to the theatre. I’m afraid Walter wouldn’t like that kind of patronage for this Sam Evans.”

“ O, Fred, then you do admit that there is harm in the theatre? ”

“ If that isn’t a woman’s conclusion. I said Walter wouldn’t like it, and forsooth! she charges me with having said I thought there was harm in it. Still, we may as well have it out; for I have been waiting and wondering whether I should venture to ask you to go there or to the opera. The season is fairly under way now, and you know you promised to think the matter over.”

“ And I’ve kept my promise, Fred. But I have not quite made up my mind yet. I want to ask you a question or two, and Sam

Evans' case is just in point. Admitting that going to the theatre has never harmed you, and might never harm me; admitting that we have both home influences of a kind to counteract the effect that might be hurtful; and even admitting that we are proof against the danger of indulging too often in that kind of amusement, I wish you would tell me whether you think Sam, and the thousands of others like him, young men, in boarding houses, and in business here, with no home influences whatever to restrain them, are likely to stop at a safe point, —if safe point there be?"

"Well, of course, not so likely."

"Well, another thing, Fred. In the case of Sam, who would, at first, at least go alone, or with fellow-clerks, — I mean not with ladies, — are there many steps between the theatres and the drinking shops? Are there not men hanging about the theatres

who would be likely to tempt him in to
drink, or to gamble, probably to do both? "

" O, of course. There are sharpers all
about to make a fellow drink and gamble.
But you know we were discussing Margaret
Worthington and the effect of the theatre
upon her. You would not go from the theatre to a gambling saloon. And if you go
with me, I promise to come straight home
with you, without going after any sharpers."

And he laughed.

" That would be satisfactory, perhaps, if
I were only accountable for myself. But
the responsibility of one human being for
another's way of living has pressed fearfully
upon me lately, Fred."

" My dear Mag! I think that is going
too far entirely. If I look after myself, I
think that is quite enough. And if you are
not afraid of being injured by the theatre,
I don't believe you need refuse to go be-

cause Sam Evans, or any other man, goes
and gets drunk afterwards. That's his lookout, not yours or mine."

"But, Fred, I know you are wrong.
It is my lookout, and yours, too."

"How, pray?"

"Why you know what St. Paul said
about the meat?"

"I'm sure I don't."

"'If meat make my brother to offend, I
will eat no meat while the world standeth,
lest I make my brother to offend.' I begin
to see, Fred, that the question of influence
and example is enough to keep me away.
I don't really feel as if going once or twice,
or perhaps occasionally, to see fine plays
finely acted, would do me or any one else
any harm. But if Sam should see me once at
a first-class theatre, (I take Sam as a repre-
sentative case,) I should have no right to
expect him to argue that I did not go

oftener, and to all sorts of theatres. I would rather not have him able to say, ' She goes, and why may not I? ' If I err in not going, I am sure to err on the safe side."

Fred bit his lips. " You are like a stone wall; and I have to be silenced if not convinced. And now for the opera."

" I am going to do a strange thing about that, Fred. I have just decided upon a plan. I don't really understand the difference between the effects of going to the theatre and going to the opera. And so I am going to ask you to take me to the opera the first night you choose."

" Hurrah for Mag! " was Fred's exclamation of delight.

" Hush, Fred! I have not finished. I don't promise ever to go more than the once. I know I should enjoy it. But I believe that strength has been given me,—

for indeed, Fred, this has been no trifling matter to me, and I have wanted to avoid all conflict, and go everywhere with you all,— but I do believe strength has been given me to decide by my conscience rather than by my inclination. I am going once, and then I shall be able to argue more intelligently on the subject."

"Going as a sort of metaphysical experiment?"

"Going to see just what it is, and how it strikes me. If I decide against it, you will let me abide by my decision, Fred?"

"Don't quite see how I can help it," was the answer. "You are too good for us, Mag; that's the trouble with you. But somehow it's rather becoming; and I don't know that a depth of iniquity would suit your style."

"O Fred! you wouldn't call me good if you knew me."

"Wouldn't I? Well, I hope I shan't make your acquaintance then. I rather like to consider you good, if it does make you lose some treats." And he kissed her before he went off.

She sat down, at once, and wrote to Walter a letter full of sympathy with his interest in Sam Evans. And then she detailed the conversation which had followed Fred's reading of the letter.

"I do love Fred dearly," she said, "and he seems really to be fond of me. And O, Walter, it is so sad to see his trifling way of looking at matters. He is light-hearted about everything, for he has never had any trouble in his life. And he rushes into all sorts of things, without stopping to think about them. I wish you could be with him. Your clear head and your ballast might help him. I feel so powerless. I hope I have done right in promising to go once to the

opera. But it is very hard for me to get a
clear light upon these things. Fred's exult-
ant exclamation made me a little bit afraid
that I was compromising matters. I do so
want to do him good, that I look anxiously
for the effect of everything I do or say.
And of one thing I am very sure, he is
studying me as a sort of curiosity. I know
he watches me closely, and I need to guard
myself very carefully. I want him to see
in me a thoroughly unflinching, determined
Christian; and I also want him to see how
happy a Christian necessarily is. Of course
any one would be happy in the main, with
every one petting one, and trying to make
life pleasant. But I want Fred to see that
the peace which passeth all understanding
keeps one happy of itself, and is beyond
the reach of accessories. I want him to
know that I could be happy, as God helping
me I could, even if he called me to pass

through trials. I want to show this to all of them here. The girls puzzle me exceedingly. I sometimes think that Kitty would do anything but repel me, if I spoke to her. And I cannot help feeling that Laura is far from being at rest. It is very hard to know whether to speak or not. Frank is a noble fellow. Naturally, I think he is more earnest than Fred. He is very ambitious, and studies hard. I think he has a fine mind. Sue is a real comfort. I teach her Bible verses every day with her lessons, now; and her comments and questions are very bright, but sadly like those a bright little heathen might ask. Fred has promised to call on Sam for me, and I think if we can get him really interested in lending Sam a helping hand, it may be a new illustration of the waterer being watered."

Meanwhile, Fred had hastened to report

to Laura and Kitty Margaret's position respecting the theatre and the opera.

" Now which opera shall we take her to see?" he asked. " It must be one of the very finest; for I am determined she shall enjoy it thoroughly."

" And it must be one of the entirely unexceptionable ones," said Laura; " for I don't want it to frighten her away."

" Do you really want her to yield in these points? " said Kitty.

" Why of course," was the immediate reply from both Laura and Fred.

" Well, do you know I am not so sure that I do? There is a difference between us, and I do believe Mag's life is the most satisfying. She is so holy, somehow," Kitty added, with a sort of awe in her voice, " that I think of her as something a little above us. And I would rather the distance would be lessened by our growing up to her, than by her coming towards us.”

“ She means all she says,” said Fred. “ That’s the point that makes me willing she should have her own way. And the points she has a tender conscience about are the only ones in which she takes a stand. No one in the world was ever more yielding where just her own convenience or pleasure is concerned. O, if all members of the church were like her I don’t believe I would quarrel with any of them. But then, — ”

“ Well, she certainly has champions in you and Kitty,” said Laura. “ And Father and Mother and the others are just the same. It must be that I’m a great deal worse than anybody else, that such exceeding goodness don’t suit me. I don’t like to look at other people’s consciences; and Margaret’s is so perpetually in the foreground. I love her dearly over our lessons, or walks, or music, or, — any time but when these subjects are broached. And then it makes me savage. I can't tell you how I feel. I want to fly out of the room. And although she has not once, in the last two months she has been here, said one word to me, whatever she may have done to you, it keeps me in a perfect fidget whenever I am alone with her. I'm so afraid she'll preach."

They went to the opera before many nights had passed, Margaret with very mingled feelings. She was sometimes afraid she was doing wrong; at others, convinced that she was doing right. Her cousins were determined to make the evening charming, and they appeared to succeed. Margaret was very quiet and listened very intently. And the decision that the one visit led her to she imparted to Emily as follows:

"I have been to the opera, dear, as I

wrote you that I intended going. And I think that you will never hear me say that again. I have told Uncle Henry and the rest that I cannot make it seem right to go with them, and they are all very good and very lovely, and will not press me any further. And I have an idea that in their hearts they would a little rather have heard this decision from me than any other. Perhaps I am mistaken, but that has nothing to do with it. Well, Emily, the opera is, undoubtedly, fascinating. The mere fact of the brilliantly-lighted house, and the gayly-dressed audience, is an excitement. And the music was, oh! so exquisite. You know my love of music. And my fear in going was, that it might make me forget to look calmly at the question of right or wrong connected with it. I prayed very earnestly before I went, and I do not think it was running wrongly into temptation. At all

events, I did not forget. I sent up a great
many little prayers while I was there, and
I am so satisfied with the result, to my own
mind, that I do not think I did wrong. I
do not think my visit has harmed me. The
plot of the opera was not as bad as a great
many novels that are circulated now-a-days,
though that did not make it good. I do
not know whether it was purer than others,
or not. I am sure a perpetual indulgence
in such distracting enjoyments would be hurtful. But I do not think an occasional visit
need do one any harm, if it could be taken
apart from all its accessories. But I saw
enough in my one visit, of blasè men and
fast-looking women, to make me feel that
this was one of their rallying points. And
I am sure that Satan's strongholds are not
the best places for the assembling of Christians. Then, the opera may do harm. And
if I, by going, induce another to go, or

even countenance his going, and he is harmed by it, am I not responsible, to no small degree? Could I bear to have any one confess that the opera had driven away serious thoughts, if it had done nothing more, and at the same time assert that he had met me there, knowing my profession, and so he had supposed there was no wrong in it? And then, what I think really impressed me most, was the effect that such a life must have upon actors and actresses. I cannot tell you how that shocked me. It was a view of the case that had never urged itself upon me before; but it overwhelmed me, as through the evening I realized more and more fully the temptations to which they must be exposed. That lovely-looking, pretty prima donna, with that wonderfully thrilling voice, — I pitied her so. Do you know I cannot help praying for her? O, dear Emily, the more I think of it, the

more sure I am that professing Christians
had better keep away from such places. I
would rather my brothers should see me
take this stand. And I do believe that at
the last day we will look more freely in
our Saviour's face; will go to him with
garments more ‘ unspotted from the world,’
if we draw our line of separation this side
of the opera. We are to be a ‘ peculiar
people’— to separate ourselves. And after
all, it is not very much to give up for Him
who bought us with His precious blood.
There may be some, even among Christians,
who will think me too strict; but I think
they will be in the minority. Even if they
were not, my decision would have to abide.
I feel sure that I shall never regret it.
Had I decided otherwise, how bitterly I
might have had to repent. So the matter,
and all like conflicts, are at an end. I have
assumed my position definitely, at last, be-

fore the family; and they are all so good to me, it made it all the harder to oppose their wishes. Laura and Fred seem to feel the matter most. Laura is a little bit, just a little bit, scornful. My great fear concerning her is that she will think me Pharisaical. But she is such a dear cousin; and in all our studies, and every day pursuits, we are so completely one, I do not think I shall lose her love. Fred is hurt and annoyed, and yet very forgiving, and seems all the more eager to provide such amusements as I can enjoy. Kitty's great maxim is to let all the world have its own way. She can't bear to interfere with people's idiosyncrasies. The world is big enough for her and every one beside; and she has a happy faculty for avoiding all collisions. And taken as a whole, their sense of courtesy, and true politeness, would forbid their urging upon a guest anything disagreeable or

objectionable. You see I have not had anything to endure. And I end as I began, —
they are all so good to me. O, Emily, pray,
pray for them with all your might; for it
has become a necessity to me to see them
Christians.”

“ Kitty,” said Laura, that same day,
“ does this obstinacy come from Margaret’s
religion? She used to be such a yielding,
pliable creature.”

“ You call it obstinacy? ” cried Kitty.
“ Well, it’s a sort of obstinacy that one
can’t help admiring. Come, Laura, confess. Is it not true that it’s only exhibited
when she has really made up her mind to a
matter of principle? She is anything but
obstinate about all other things. Laura, I
do think, taken all in all, she is the most
perfect character I ever saw. She always
was lovely, but she is different; and if it is

joining the church that made her so, I don't
see why we don't all do it."

" That's just like you, Kitty," Laura answered. " You cannot love a person in a
rational manner; you must rush into enthusiasm. I do love Margaret dearly; and of
course she has a right to her own opinions.
And I am happy to say she don't try to
force them on other people. But I do not
see why she need want to seem better than
other people. And besides, I don't suppose
she would herself attribute it to joining the
church. I suppose it's a change, of some
kind, inside; and that might come without
the other."

" I don't know much about it, to be
sure," said Kitty. " But I don't want to
die just yet. For apart from my satisfaction with my present condition, I do
believe, Laura, that I might be better
prepared."

"O, Kitty, do stop." Laura could bear it no longer. "You dear old Kit, you are just right as you are; and I'm sure you don't look at all likely to die. Don't get your head full of these things, Kitty, don't." And Laura put both arms around Kitty, as if she feared the opening of a great gulf between them. And after that the sisters separated for the night, neither of them quite at rest. Kitty was indeed beginning to long for inward peace, which, in spite of all her joyousness, was wanting in her soul. Laura was only disturbed; at what, she hardly knew. In both hearts seed had been sown; into both leaven had entered, though neither really knew it.

Margaret, meanwhile, longed and prayed and watched her own life jealously; but she had never yet spoken. She was afraid of giving offence; of injuring the cause she would fain advance; of appearing intrusive;

and of barring the way to further confidence. It is well to be very, very careful;
to choose carefully and prayerfully our time
to speak the word in season. But let us
be just as watchful, lest we mistake our
own cowardice for prudence; reluctance for
wisdom. Is it not generally true, that when
we go to a friend with a message from the
Master; go armed with his words and not
our own; go trusting his strength to counteract our weakness; his power to overrule
our helplessness.— we find that He has prepared the way for us, and made ready the
ground? Are we not often welcomed where
we had feared to be repelled? So those
who have tried most often have testified.
So Margaret found it, when at last she could
bear her anxiety no longer.

CHAPTER XVI.

Margaret's interest in her Sabbath School class grew from week to week. Her cousins declared that it was becoming the main object of her existence, though this was an exaggeration; for she determined not to let it stand between her and the demands her cousins choose to make upon her time. She had won the boys' hearts utterly. The superintendent no longer thought of that corner as the centre of all disturbance; for although Margaret's brain and heart and often physical strength were taxed to the utmost, in trying to control them, she generally succeeded. The boys really cared for her; and seeing that noise or inattention made her look sad and care-worn, they suppressed their desires for fun, and usually listened to what she said. She found her way to the forlorn tenements which these boys called their homes. And after her first visit, her only wonder was that the boys were not a great deal worse. She heard the details of their every day life. She learned to know something of the temptations which assailed them in their workshops. She was brought face to face with poverty more intense than she had previously imagined; with sickness, so hard to bear at all times, so fearfully aggravated when there is no money wherewith to meet the demands which it makes; when the loss of a single working day means just so much less food for a family. She saw life in many new phases, and oh! how she longed for power to give relief; how she longed to have the veil removed, and the light of the Holy Ghost sent into these dark, dark places. She toiled and she prayed. And she had great comfort in the thought that she was not alone in her work. Emily was always full of interest and sympathy. And Aunt Dinah and Miss Harriet and Miss Chryssie could not hear enough of Margaret's doings.

"Do tell her not to be discouraged," Miss Chryssie said. "I am so glad she has boys to teach. May be our Charlie left a boy somewhere in New York."

"Tell Miss Marget I prays for them are boys of hern," said Aunt Dinah. "I can't do nothin' else for my Master, but I ken pray for those as is doin'."

And never did messages carry more refreshment than these and many others like them. She kept her class throughout her stay. And though when she left it she dared not say that a single one had come to Christ, there were some who seemed to her to have started in the upward path. And the harvest came, as come it always will when the seed is sown in faith, even though one may sow and another may reap. Months afterwards she heard of fruit in the very place where she least would have expected it.   And for what was not given to her eyes to see, she had faith to wait till the day when all things shall be revealed, and to stay herself on the promise, " My word shall not return unto me void."   " Ye know that your labor is not in vain in the Lord."

Of former work she saw some blessed result.   Frank coming abruptly into the library one day, surprised Margaret, open letter in hand, and eyes full of tears.

"No bad news, I hope, Margery?" he asked, somewhat alarmed.

"O no, Frank; the best of news. My letter is from one of my Rowenah Sunday School. I don't know why I began to cry, for it has made me very happy.''

"Why, what's up?"

"I don't know that you would care much, Frank, but read the letter if you want to.''

His curiosity was roused, and he took it.

"Dear, dear Miss Worthington:

I must tell you how happy I am. I have not forgotten my promise to pray and read the Bible and try to be a Christian. And I do think, Miss Worthington, that Jesus has heard my prayers and forgiven my sins. I have told Him just how sinful I am, and how I know that nothing but His blood can save me. And I do think He has saved me. Miss

Worthington, it was you that made me think about it; and I do love you and thank you so very much. And, Miss Worthington, do you think I might make so bold as to ask Dr. Robinson to let me join the church? O, I want to so much. I want to obey Jesus's last command; and I want to let everybody know that I am His disciple. It ain't that I think I'm fit, but you said we didn't need to be fit. I wish you were here, you would tell me just what to do. Won't you please write to me? And if you would, if you think I may join the church, write and tell Dr. Robinson that I want to talk to him, so that I won't have to tell him all myself. Dear Miss Worthington, I do love you ever so much. And O, won't you please pray for me, and help me all you can, for I know I am very weak and sinful.   Your loving scholar,

ELIZA WOOD."

Frank handed back the letter, and said:

"There's one thing certain, Margery, all sorts of people love you. And if this makes you glad, why I'm glad, too."

" I thank you, Frank. And O, Frank, if you only would ask the Saviour yourself. I can't help saying it, Frank. You don't know how much I think about it. Won't you, Frank?"

He was a good deal astonished, but he only said:

" Do you care so much, Margie? Do you really think it makes so much difference?"

" O Frank, if you only knew,—if I could only tell you what a difference!"

" Well, I suppose I ought to think about it, and would like to please you. May be I will try."

" If you begin to do it to please me, you will soon do it for your own sake, I am sure."

The months were flitting on. Thanksgiving had passed, and Christmas was at hand. Mr. Chauncey had fulfilled his promise of making the winter a happy one to Margaret. Her lessons were progressing even to the satisfaction of her high ambition; and the amusements in which she did participate she entered upon with a keen relish. But the greatest treat of all was in store for her yet. One day, just before dinner, she had been out alone visiting some of her Sabbath School scholars, and as she approached the house she saw Kitty, her face all a-glow, at the window, evidently waiting for her. She went up the steps in a wondering sort of way. Before she could touch the bell the door flew open, as if by invisible means. She peered behind it, expecting to see Kitty, and behold, — Walter and Rob. She was absolutely speechless for a moment; but the boys had full use of their faculties, and she

was greeted with loving words, kisses, em-
braces, and finally dragged into the parlor,
from which her uncle's family had been
watching her face, as the expression changed
from blank amazement to unbounded satisfaction.

" Is this some of your goodness, Uncle
Henry? " and she released herself from the
boys' grasp and went to him.

" Yes," cried Kitty. " Only think of
Papa having had a secret, sly plan of his
own, and not even telling Mamma."

 " You did not know, Aunt Alice? "

" Never dreamed of such a thing, dear;
and what is more, I didn't recognize my
own nephews when they appeared. Laura
and I were sitting here with callers, and
these two young gentlemen were ushered in.
I hadn't the least idea who they were. I
thought Walter and Rob were little boys."

" Well," said Uncle Henry, " I thought

that for once we would have a regular jol-
lification for the holidays; and I wanted
your father and mother to come, too.''

'' Oh ! '' and Mag's exclamation was a
curious combination of gratitude to her
uncle, and disappointment that his plan had
not succeeded.

'' Papa is so busy over his book,'' ex-
plained Walter. '' He said he must work
this vacation; and Mamma would not leave
him, of course.''

'' Well, Mag, dinner is ready, and you
are not. The boys won't go home to-
night,'' urged saucy Fred.

She started up stairs; but the boys could
not let her go. One posted himself on one
side, the other on the other; and Fred stood
at the foot of the stairs laughing.

'' I say, Margery, did you notice that
Papa asked Sam Evans to come in this evening; he expected a friend whom he would

like to have him meet; and not one of us had the curiosity to ask him whom he meant?"

"Why, neither we did. How strange! I meant to, but I was talking to Mr. Montgomery at the time, and it passed from my mind afterwards."

"O, to be sure. Mr. Montgomery is responsible for a good many forgets, is he not, Margaret?"

"Fred, for shame! Wait till I come down, and I'll ask after Miss Walliston." And she went into her own room. .

"O, boys, how good it is to see you! When did you make up your mind to come?"

"Got a letter from Uncle Henry on Saturday; and here we are on Thursday. Emily's been working herself sick every moment since, making some Christmas present or other; it's in our trunk, with Papa's and Mamma's."

"Sam Evans is doing so well, Walter. The firm is so pleased with him."

"I am so thankful. And you must read his letters. He thinks this house is a sort of Paradise, and you girls not much short of angels. Are you ready? Come, let's go down."

The fortnight that followed was one long dream of happiness to our friends. Sightseeing and pleasuring occupied them, and many long talks, — the interchange of much which had not been, and never could be, put on paper, — and the complete sealing of friendship and intimacy between the two families of cousins. Laura and Walter grew confidential at once. Kitty and Rob were proverbial for their flow of spirits, and were the leaders in a charade party which passed off with great eclat; and Margaret

was the very personification of ecstasy, all
the time.

But the last day of their visit came. And
the climax to all their frolics was succeeded
by what had nearly been a sorrow to cloud
perpetually the memories of that merry
group. The frolic was a moonlight sleigh-
ride to the Park. It was a night made for
them, Fred said. Full moon, crisp snow,
fresh horses, — a gayer party never set out.
It was so glorious that they were tempted
far beyond the Park. Their bells rang, in
concert with many others, up the Blooming-
dale road, till High Bridge was reached;
and not until they turned did they notice
clouds, which had arisen suddenly, and which
were fast gathering nearer and nearer to the
moon, till its light was completely obscured.
Alas, for our treacherous New York cli-
mate! In a few moments a drizzling rain
was falling, which soon increased, and they

reached home amid hail and sleet and wet snow, — "A nasty storm," Fred called it.

It would have taken more than that to dampen their spirits, however. And the hot oysters and coffee which Mr. Chauncey had provided soon relieved the chilliness of all but Laura, who said she had never felt coldness penetrate her as it had done; she was sure that nothing but bed would warm her; and there she went, her teeth chattering, and no amount of wrapping seeming to avail anything. Still no one realized that she was going to be ill. And when Margaret and Kitty left her they thought, and she herself hoped, that a night's rest would fully restore her. But when Kitty hastened to her, in the morning, she found fever written on her face; and she had to confess that she was so stiff, with such strange pains in every limb, that she could not rise.

Kitty was dismayed. Sickness was a thing almost unknown in their household, and she did not comprehend it. She summoned her mother, and the doctor was soon there. The boys had to leave, their college term being about to begin, but they went off, anxious faces and heavy hearts testifying to the sad termination of their merriment. That snow-storm and many another passed away, and spring flowers were venturing forth from their winter resting-places before Laura crossed again the threshold of her room. Inflammatory rheumatism, of the most severe nature, settled upon her frame. And there were long days and nights when life and death seemed so nearly balanced that the weight of a hair might have turned the scale.

Kitty said many times during those weeks, and always afterwards, that she could never have lived through them but for Margaret.

They divided between them the most arduous labors of the sick-room, for Aunt Alice
was by no means strong; and no observer
could have told which was the sister and
which the cousin of the invalid. Margaret
was thoughtful, noiseless, tender, unweary-
ing, — the very model of a nurse, — and
outside of the room was the one who hoped
almost against hope; who carried the first
news of change for the better to the anxious
brothers; who never allowed them to feel
the loneliness which the monoply of the
sick-room might have caused; who insisted
that Kitty, whose nerves were strung to
their tensest reach, should take necessary
rest, lulling her to sleep sometimes as if
she had been a weary child; who thought
of all the others before she thought of herself. And all the time she was praying,
praying, praying, that God would not take
Laura away unprepared: that he would, at

least, restore her mind, which so often wandered, and give them comfort as to her future life, if die she must; and that Kitty
should be led to look away from all frail
earthly helpers, in this hour of greater need
than she ever yet had known, to Him who
had loved her with an everlasting love, and
who now was only waiting for her to arise
and go to her Father: ready, while she was
yet a great way off, to hasten to her. Nor
were her prayers unanswered.

There came one Sabbath when anxiety
about Laura reached its height. The fever
had kept her in a delirious condition all day
long. The rheumatism was very near her
heart. The doctor dared not bid them hope.
The house was hushed and still. Dr. Harris
called after church, and had seen Mr. Chauncey and Fred; all other visitors were ex-
cluded. The day wore on, how, they
scarcely knew. Laura had ceased to recog-

nize even her mother; and the shadow of
death seemed actually upon them. Kitty
had kept herself as calm as possible; but late
in the afternoon, when Laura called for her
in reproachful tones, fancying herself de-
serted, she could bear it no longer, and she
burst into such fearful sobbing that they had
to lead her from the room. She could not
check herself, and Mr. Chauncey had to use
tones of real command, and to send her to
bed, promising to call her at the slightest
change. Margaret assisted her to undress,
and Kitty grew gradually calmer; but when
in bed, she clung to Margaret and said:

"Don't leave me, O don't leave me,
Margie! There is nothing you can do for
Laura, and I must have you."

"Darling, I will stay just as long as you
want me," Mag tenderly replied. "But
ought you not to sleep?"

"I couldn't sleep, indeed I could not.

O, Mag, do you think Laura will really die?"

"Dear Kitty, I cannot give up hope. She is in God's hands, and He will do what is best for her."

"But O, Mag," and her voice fell so that Margie could hardly hear, "do you think she is fit to die? do you pray for her, Mag?"

The first question was too hard to answer, and the second surprised Mag.

"Kitty, I pray all the time for her, darling, and for all of us."

"O, Margie, I am not fit to die!"

"I pray for you, too, Kitty; not only now, but always. And it may be, darling, that this is sent to you now to make you fit. Don't cry so, Kitty; don't, dearest. Lie down and bathe your head, and I will read to you, may I, from the Bible?

"O, Margie, please do!"

And Margie hastened to get her own, with hurried prayers for wisdom to choose the right words. The spirit never turns away from such prayers. And this was the message he sent to Kitty. "When thou passeth through the waters, I will be with thee; and through the rivers, they shall not overflow thee; when thou walkest through the fire thou shalt not be burned; neither shall the flame kindle upon thee. For I am the Lord thy God, the Holy One of Israel, thy Saviour."

"That is very beautiful, Margie; but it is not for me. He is not my Saviour."

"Listen, dear. 'When the poor and needy seek water, and there is none, and their tongue faileth for thirst, I the Lord will hear them; I the God of Israel will not forsake them.'"

"But I have forsaken Him, Margie. I never cared for Him when I was happy."

"I will bring the blind by a way that they knew not; I will lead them in paths that they have not known; I will make darkness light before them, and crooked things straight. These things will I do unto them, and not forsake them."

"O, Margie, if he would only forgive me; but I am so wicked!"

"Kitty, darling, whom else did he die for? 'The Lord hath laid on Him the iniquity of us all.'"

"But I deserve to be punished. I don't deserve to be forgiven."

"'They that are whole have no need of a physician, but they that are sick. I came not to call the righteous, but sinners to repentance.' His own words, you know, Kitty."

"How sweet they are. It seems as if I had never heard them before. O, Margie, it seems strange that I do not love Him."

" Are you sure you do not, darling? He suffered and died for you. Can you help loving Him? ‘ We love Him because He first loved us.’ "

" O, Margie, I do love Him; I do want to. But how can I go to Him?’’

" Kitty, He is the way, just He alone. He died to save you, Kitty, — He died."

" Margie, Margie, how strange it all is! Of course I knew all this before, — but I never really knew it, either. Margie, Jesus loves me, — me, who have never cared the least bit for Him. But I do care now. How dreadful it seems to feel happy when Laura is so ill. And yet I do feel happy. Jesus has forgiven my sins. And perhaps Laura will get well yet. If she does, — O Margie, even if she does not, I must believe and love and serve Him all my days. Ask Him to help me, Margie."

And Margie closed the door and offered a

simple little prayer, and could not but be surprised at the calmness and peace which had taken the place of Kitty's excitement. The light had come. The crooked ways were straight. She trusted Christ for herself; and she was willing to trust Him for her sister.

"You need not stay now, dear; only please leave me your Bible a little while. Can't you go and rest? I have worn you out more than even Laura."

"O, Kitty, I am so thankful; so happy. Jesus is so good." And with a long, fervent embrace, she left her.

Kitty knelt down alone, and yet she did not know what to say. She had not prayed for years, excepting for Laura's life. And now it seemed as if she must pray incessantly. She was like a little child; just as trustful, and just as timid. But she there made the solemn covenant with her Saviour, from which she never swerved. Christ was henceforth her chosen portion, and she was His child.

The change may seem to some too sudden to be real. And yet God does sometimes lead His chosen ones in just such ways. Kitty had, for years, known what she ought to believe. There was no need of long doctrinal training; no need of long stumbling in dark mazes. She felt her need of help. She knew who was the helper. And the sense of need, the cry for assistance, and the answer of life-giving strength, were almost simultaneous. When she went down to tea all wondered at her calmness, little dreaming whence it flowed. But her frank, impulsive nature was still her own. And she took an opportunity to follow her father, as he passed sadly into his library, his heart very heavy on account of his eldest child. He sat down without observing her, and rested his head upon his hand. She touched him softly.

"Papa, I want to tell you something."

"Well, darling," and he looked up at her there. "Papa, I have found out to-day how wicked I have been all my life," — and she paused, — "and, Papa, I have asked Jesus to forgive me, and I believe He has done it. I love Him so, Papa. I must serve Him all the rest of my life."

Mr. Chauncey was much moved.

"My child, God bless you," he said. "I am well satisfied to have it so."

"And O, Papa," and her eyes filled, "I do believe He will save poor Laura. That He will not take her away from us."

And the flood-gates were once more opened. Her father folded her in his arms. She wept for some time, but much more silently than in the afternoon, and then kissed him and went up stairs.

Margaret had been busy with Laura, and was just coming down to her tea. Kitty met her in the hall.

"I have told Papa," she whispered to Margaret. And Margaret could not but look at her in surprise.

She was so retiring herself that it had been very hard to speak, even to her parents, from whom she was so sure of a welcome and glad reception. And that Kitty should have gone at once, and with very little time for forethought, to her Uncle Henry, seemed marvelous.

"And what did he say?"

"That he was well satisfied. O, Margery, I wonder if he is not a Christian? You pray for him, don't you?"

"Indeed I do."

"How strange it seems that I have lived so long without praying. I feel as if I must do it all the time now."

Fred took Mag to the dining-room, and helped her to her tea; and she lingered with him for awhile afterwards.

"Sam Evans was here while you were with Kitty, this afternoon; and I happened to open the door for him."

"Did you? Did he want anything especial?"

"No; only to ask how Laura was. He is very full of sympathy for us."

"He's a good-hearted fellow."

"Yes, he is; I like him. And I guess he has sown all his wild oats."

"Well, you have had a good deal to do with it, then, Fred. I must tell you what he told Walter. I have thought of it ever so often; but we have all been so engrossed with Laura that I have had no opportunity to tell you. He said he owed a great deal to you. That you had kept him out of bad company, and introduced him to people who wouldn't do him any harm; and that he never would forget it."

"Pshaw! I haven't done anything. That is, I wouldn't have, but for you and Walter's letter. You see the good deeds all spring, originally, from you."

"But I could never have accomplished what you have."

"Well, now I'll tell you what you have done. Sam told me, one night, that he did love the theatre dearly, and I said:

"Well, I don't see the harm of going to see good acting, Evans. You needn't go and get drunk after it, and plenty of good people go."

"'I want to ask you something, Chauncey,' he said. 'Does Miss Worthington go?'"

"No," I said.

"'And do you know why?' he asked.

"Well, I tried to quote you, though I
19

made a queer botch of it, I expect. However, I made him understand your notions about example and all that. And when he took it in, he said:

" ' Well, I know nothing could harm her; and if she stays away for fear of hurting such fellows as I am, I guess I'd better not trust myself to go. I don't care to get quite as low down as I was.' "

" So, Margie, if that's any compensation to you, you can have the credit of keeping him out of what you consider dangerous ground."

" Indeed, it is a satisfaction. And I don't believe you are sorry I did not go."

" I don't say anything about that."

But he might have said a good deal if he had uttered all his thoughts.

After Margaret had gone up stairs, he sauntered into the library. His father was reading, and Fred saw that he had the Bible.

“ Why, Father, is Laura worse? ”

“ No, Fred ; ” and he started up. “ What do you mean? Did they call me?”

“ O no, sir ; I only thought,” — he was afraid to say what he thought, but he looked at the open Bible, and his father felt with a keen sense of shame the astonishment which accompanied the look.

“ You are astonished at my choice of a book, Fred. But I begin to think I ought to have read it more than I have. When death comes so near our door it seems as if we needed something that can conquer it, and there is nothing in this world strong enough for that. Kitty has found it out, it seems.”

“ Sir? ”

“ Kitty has been to me to-night. She is following in Margery’s footsteps, it appears.”

“ You don’t mean that she is going to be religious, Father? ”

"She must serve Christ all the rest of her life, she says. And I would not have it otherwise."

"But, Father, what does it mean? Is she just frightened and blue about Laura?"

"I wish you had seen her face, Fred. She did not look like one who had been frightened into anything. And as to the 'blue,' — there has not been such a happy face in this house since you went on the ride which has cost our dear Laura so much."

The entrance of the Doctor interrupted them. He had just been to Laura's room.

"I am glad to say, Mr. Chauncey, that I think I have reason to consider Miss Laura's symptoms a little more favorable to-night. She is very, very ill, yet; and a little change may turn the scale back again; but there is a glimmer more of hope than I could perceive this morning."

"I am truly thankful to hear you say even that, Doctor. Has the fever abated?"

"Her pulse is lower; but her mind is still wandering. She is well cared for, though, and that is almost everything in such a case. That niece of yours is a treasure, sir. I have seldom seen her equal in a sick room."

The "treasure" herself was in the room as the Doctor's words passed his lips.

"Dear Uncle Henry! O, Fred!" she exclaimed. "Laura opened her eyes just now, and knew us all. She even asked for you, Uncle Henry!"

The Doctor and Mr. Chauncey hastened up stairs. It was indeed so. The worst of Laura's long illness was over, — the most alarming portion, at least. There were many hours of suffering yet before. The convalescence was very tedious. But the answers to inquiring friends became more and more favorable ; and joy and gladness gradually resumed their sway in the house from which they had, so for long a time, been banished.

CHAPTER XVII.

A week from that Sabbath evening Margaret and Kitty were again together.

" What a week this has been to me, Mag. The happiest week of my life."

" If I could only tell you how glad your happiness makes me."

" Margery, I must tell you that I owe it, in a great measure, to you."

" O, Kitty, I cannot see how."

" Margery, you must let me speak. You don't know what your life has been to me this winter. I never cared how I lived before, as long as I was happy. I liked to see others happy, too. But it was in a selfish sort of way; just because it made me uncomfortable to witness suffering. They might be as unhappy as they chose, if they were out of my sight. But you were so different; so, — don't interrupt me, — so unselfish; and then, so conscientious. I watched you well, Mag. And I tell you, you don't know how it would have hurt me to see you fail. I was real glad you kept the position you assumed about amusements. Perhaps I would not have got any further if Laura had not been ill. But if she had been ill before you came, I doubt if I should have got so far. O, Margie, how wonderfully the Saviour has led me."

"Just as He leads us all, Kitty."

"Now let us read together, Mag. There is so much for me to find out in the Bible that I never knew before. Show me something very full of thanksgiving, please, Margie.”

Margaret turned to the 116th Psalm, and then to the twelfth of Isaiah; and after that, to the third of Ephesians. At the twentieth verse Kitty paused.

“ Exceeding abundantly above all that we can ask or think,” she repeated.

“ Isn’t that just my case, Mag? O, I hope I shall live a long, long time. I want to do so much for Christ. Think of the years that I have lost.”

“ Dear Kitty! He forgives you for all those. Do you remember that wonderful verse? I don’t think there is a more wonderful one. ‘ Thou hast cast all my sins behind thy back.’ It is part of Hezekiah’s song of thanksgiving, when his life had been prolonged.”

“ It is wonderful, Margie. It means that He not only forgives, but forgets, does it not? Casts them behind his back, out of sight; covers them over with His blood? O, how strange that I never knew it before! O, how I wish the others all felt the same! What can I do to show them, Margie?"

"Pray without ceasing, dear, first of all. And then, live so that they shall see Jesus in your life. And one great thing, I think, is to let people see that we are the happiest creatures in the world. That we have a source of joy of which they know nothing, and which never fails in the most adverse outward circumstances. For the certainty of being always happy will often attract people when nothing else will."

"But what about speaking to them?"

"That will come, of course, when a fit opportunity occurs. But I really think the other two are often more important. And especially in such a case as yours, where they all know everything that you can tell them about their duty.”

“ Dear Margaret, how you do help me ! ”

“ Girls,” and Aunt Alice’s head appeared at the door, “ Laura is awake now, and feels a little more comfortable. Fred and Frank are with her, and she wants you, too.”

She looked very ill to them yet ; but the change within a week was marked. She was fearfully thin ; and her face bore traces of the suffering that was racking her frame, which not even her loving smile of welcome could banish. She could not extend her hand to them, and the kisses that they showered upon her fell very gently, for the lightest pressure gave her pain.

“ Sit where I can see you, please. How strange it is that I should have been so ill. How long ago the sleigh-ride seems. What’s the news from the boys, Mag?’’

" They are well, dear; and so glad to hear that you are better. Their letters have been so anxious. Walter says he could hardly bear to think of your suffering."

They sat there for half an hour, Laura too weak to do much more than listen to their quiet talk, her countenance lighting up, however, with something like its own expression at some of Fred's sallies.

Kitty was rather more quiet than was her wont. She sat just where the fire-light could play over her face; and as it danced and glowed, the gas being turned quite low, Laura watched her, and thought she had never seen Kitty look so radiant.

When they were about to separate, her mother intending to remain with her for the night, one after another kissed her; and as Kitty bent over the bed, Laura detained her.

" Wait a moment, Kitty dear. Has anything happened? "

“ What do you mean? ”

“ You look so wonderfully happy ; and yet, you are so quiet.”

“ Dear Laura, you are getting better, you know.” And the recollection of the previous Sabbath brought tears to her eyes.

“ Is that all? ”

“ I have been wondering how I should show God how thankful I am for sparing my sister.” Then fearing to excite her, she bade her good-night.

Laura was too weak to think much. But it struck her as something very strange that Kitty should be thinking of thanking God for anything.

“ It is God who has kept me, isn’t it? ” she said to herself. “ And if Kitty wants to show thankfulness, I ought to, too, I suppose. But I can’t think about it now. I must get well first. I wonder if Margaret has taken advantage of my sickness to preach, — 'improving the opportunity,' — that's the cant phrase, I believe."

Her door was open; and from the parlor came strains of music. She knew that they were singing hymns. She could not catch the words, and the melody lulled her to sleep. But if she could have known the intensity of Kitty's feelings as she sang " Just as I am," and

> "O happy day, that fixed my choice
> On thee, my Saviour and my God,"

she would not have gone to sleep, perhaps, as undisturbed in spirit as she did.

Fred and Frank watched Kitty with more understanding than did Laura; for they had both heard the change which had occurred within her. Frank had not forgotten his cousin's words. And Margaret's walk and Kitty's determination had made Fred pause and think. But alas! both the boys were lingering, delaying, willing to admit that there was something in religion for other people, but for themselves waiting for " a more convenient season."

Mrs. Chauncey was so busy with Laura still that she had scarcely thought of Kitty. On Mr. Chauncey, of all in the house, the impression was the most profound. Between him and Kitty there existed a most noticeable congeniality. She often declared that her father was her idol. And from earliest childhood she had poured her confidence first of all into his ears. To him she had gone, naturally enough, therefore, with her great news, and it had touched him very much. He knew that she had taken a step in advance of him; that she had entered upon duties which he had neglected; and he felt a sadness at the reflection that she had learned from others the lessons which he should have taught her. The near approach

of death to his first-born child had made
him realize that with all his promise for the
welfare and happiness of his family in this
world, he had taken no pains to prepare
them for the life to come. The presence
of Margaret in his household, and especially
her close resemblance to her mother, had
carried him back to his young days when
he and his sister had been one in every
thought, feeling, and pursuit. He remembered the sense of desolate separation which
had come over him when she had chosen
the Lord for her portion; and as he looked
at Kitty in her new-found happiness, he
longed to have all her sisters and brothers
follow her, as she was following Christ.
The Bible was not only opened on that first
evening; it became a daily habit with him
to turn its pages. Nor was it long before
it was indeed " the man of his counsel, the
lamp to his path."

Arthur's name has scarcely entered upon these pages. He stood rather alone in his family: not among the fairly grown-up ones, nor yet quite young enough to rank with Sue. He went through his school-boy routine of a life with a good deal of monotony, and was only partly interested in the pursuits of the family in general. Fred was his beau-ideal of a man; whatever he said, did or thought,—yes, even more,—became at once his model. He was fond of Laura and anxious for her recovery. But such a change as that which had occurred in Kitty's life was not likely to be at first remarked by him.

But Susie's quick eyes soon spied one outward difference in Kitty. She went one morning into her cousin's room, just as she had done when Margaret first reached the city.

"Cousin Mag," she said, "Kitty does

say her prayers. I saw her this morning. And she read her Bible, too, just like you do.”

“ Yes, dear; I know it.”

“ What makes her do it, Cousin Mag ? ”

“ Because she loves Jesus, Susie.”

“ Does Jesus like to have her love Him, Cousin ? ”

“ Indeed He does, darling. Don’t you remember I told you how He loved everybody, and wanted everybody to love Him? ”

“ O, yes. Little children, too, did you say ? ”

“ Yes, my pet. Little children most of all.”

“ I think He’s pretty good, Cousin Mag. He’s making Laura well pretty fast; and Nurse says she was near dying.”

“ I know she was, precious. We must all love Him for that.”

“ I guess I do love Him. Any how, I’m

going to. I'd rather be like little Samuel than like the bad boys you told me 'bout that the bears ate up."

Margaret repeated this conversation to Kitty; and she listened, new ideas drawing upon her with regard to her responsibility as an elder sister.

"O, Margery," she said, "I will strive and pray for grace to lead little Sue to follow Jesus early. What a precious thing it would be if He would let me help to prevent her from having the long wasted years to look back upon, which keep rising up before me now."

Kitty was true to her words. Henceforward Susie was her special care. She kept the goal she had fixed steadily before her. In hours of temptation, when coldness or inattention or neglect of little duties crept in, "I must be blameless before Sue, that I may win her for Jesus," was one of the strongest incentives to watchfulness. Daily she read and prayed with Sue. Carefully she helped the child correct her faults. Tenderly she held her hand in her first steppings in the heavenly road. And at last, after years of patient waiting and watching, she was the first to welcome her into the kingdom of her Master.

CHAPTER XVIII.

Dr. Harris had watched the course of Laura's illness with the tenderest solicitude. While her life was in such danger it had seemed to him as if a child of his own were in a perilous condition; and he had spent much time in prayers on her behalf. It seemed to him as if the lesson must have been sent from the great Teacher to warn them all, while in life, to make preparation for the change that might, at any time, come upon them; and he was most anxious that it should not fall unheeded to the ground.

On one or two occasions, during his many visits to the house, he had spoken to those of the family whom he had chanced to meet; and it had seemed to him that the leaven was at work in more than one heart within that household. He had them specially upon his mind as he penned a sermon which he preached, during Laura's convalescence, from those words of Christ's parting address to his disciples: " When He comes He will reprove the world * * * of sin, because they believed not in me."

The tenor of his sermon was to show that unbelief in Christ was the great condemnatory sin. That the most complete morality of life would appear in the day of judgment as absolutely nothing, if living faith were wanting. While, on the other hand, where that existed it was enough to wash away the deepest stains of sin. Nothing else would avail when the books should be opened.

Nothing else could satisfy upon a dying bed. This faith in Christ, moreover, must be more than mere intellectual belief; for that was not, of necessity, a saving grace. Christ must be acknowledged not only as the Saviour of a dying world; not only as the Son of God become incarnate; but as a personal Saviour, the mediator between God and each one's soul. This is the faith which worketh by love; this begets the love which, if a man have, he will keep Christ's words. It is all-sufficient to save; yet it will be far from making him careless as to his after life. " Shall we continue in sin that grace may abound? God forbid. How shall we, that are dead to sin, live any longer therein? Like as Christ was raised up from the dead by the glory of the Father, even so we also should walk in newness of life." Having learned to believe in Him, we shall long so to walk as to persuade others to adopt the faith which we find so precious. But if we believe not, when He comes He will reprove of sin. Earthly position and honor; a name howsoever unsullied; a life howsoever irreproachable; a disposition so warm and loving as to have gained friends innumerable; all these will avail us nothing. "He that believeth not shall be damned."

Then, with a short but very urgent appeal to each one to secure that living faith, he left the subject in the hands of Him who alone could send the arrow to its mark. The impression left on the assembly was very solemn. Men and women and children went home with earnest thoughts awakened. In some cases, alas! the Spirit's call was unheeded; the feeling was but transient. But there was more than one burden which, in consequence of those words, was left at the foot of the cross.

Mr. Chauncey went home very much

agitated. He knew that the sermon had made a special appeal to his case. He felt that he could never be as completely at rest " without God in the world," as he had been heretofore. He was " almost persuaded" to yield at once. He believed intellectually, but he had felt to-day the insufficiency of this; and he began, with his whole heart, to desire something more satisfying. He paced his library floor in an agony of thought. He turned the pages of his Bible, but no light seemed to shine forth. His sin of unbelief grew more and more monstrous as he looked deeper and deeper within himself, and yet his eyes were holden that he should not know the life, the truth, and the way. The happy faces of his children, and especially of Margaret and Kitty, were a continual reproach to him. He did not know which way to turn. He went to church in the afternoon, but he

found no peace; and the evening was spent
in the same distracting thought. Meanwhile, Margaret and Kitty were watching
him anxiously. They had seen that something had moved him, and they longed, oh!
how they longed to have him find "joy in
believing." They prayed and watched and
longed, and kept each other's faith alive by
constant references to the promises of God's
word.

It was a wakeful night to Mr. Chauncey.
His old trouble, the inconsistency of many
professing Christians, troubled him. And
the adversary was close at hand with mani-
fold doubts and temptations to suggest.
No rest came with the morning hours.
The only resolutions to which he came were
not to allow the subject to pass from his
thoughts, and to lay his doubts and fears,
his longings and his desires, before Dr.
Harris. The latter project he carried into

effect very soon. And no words can tell the joy with which his pastor greeted him when he made known his errand. Their conversation was long, and many others followed upon the first. Point after point of misgiving and of objection did Mr. Chauncey raise, and did Dr. Harris, with the help of God, remove. For days, light was withheld; but at last it came. On Saturday night Mr. Chauncey went again to Dr. Harris's study.

"My friend," said he, "I can bear this no longer. I have been trying to make myself better; to do something for myself. And I have failed, miserably failed. I see how vain the attempt is. Now I am going 'Just as I am' to Christ. I am going to prove his words : 'Whosoever will, let him come. Him that cometh I will in no wise cast out.'"

He kept his promise. The day dawned

slowly; but the sun of righteousness did finally arise. He learned soon to look with sorrow only at the fall of others. He learned that "It is an easy thing for the best to go astray." He learned to know the merit of Jesus's blood, and the utter vanity of human strength. He endeavored to let his light so shine before men, that seeing his good works they might give all the glory to his Father in heaven.

It was from Mr. Chauncey that Dr. Harris first learned how Kitty had found her Saviour. He of course lost no time in calling upon her. He found her just as happy as we at first saw her. Clouds and shadows seemed to have no place in Kitty's horizon. All was lightness and brightness to herself and others wherever she appeared. It was beautiful to watch her kindling eye, as she spoke with a freedom from reserve at which most would marvel, of her perpetual gladness in the presence of the Saviour. And Dr. Harris saw that she was indeed "a new creature in Christ Jesus." He therefore reminded her of the communion season which would soon approach, and found that she was eagerly awaiting an opportunity to commemorate her Master's dying love.

"You think I may come so soon, Doctor? I was afraid perhaps I ought to wait till I had proved my sincerity; and I do so long to profess Christ at once. And besides, I am afraid Rowenah will claim Margaret very soon; and if you knew all she has been to me, you would not wonder that I want her with me when that joyful day comes."

"I see no reason for delay, my child. You do not profess to be perfect, else you might need to wait long enough. You only profess to have accepted the atonement of Christ offered for your sins; to have made

His righteousness your plea with your God. Why should you linger?   Would only that more of your family might be with you.''

He did not dare tell her how much hope he had with regard to her father.   His visit took place after their first interview; and Kitty did not know that they had conversed about such matters.   So she only replied:

" O, Dr. Harris, I feel as if I could not wait patiently till they come.   It seems so strange to have a joy which they cannot share; and not to be able to give it to them myself.   It is the very first feeling in my life in which I have not had full sympathy from Laura; and I am lonely without it."

Dr. Harris saw Laura that same day, for the first time since her illness.   But he found her very unwilling to allow him to make mention of Christ's name to her.   So that he had to content himself with renewed prayers.   Poor Laura!   It was through fiery trials and dreary mazes ·that the Shepherd led his lost sheep to the fold.

When Mr. Chauncey at last found the rest for which he had sighed, his joy was very different from Kitty's ecstasy. He was calm, thankful, satisfied as to his own condition; but a burden of fearful responsibility rested upon him as he looked upon his family. His anxiety for them, heightened by his sense of having been derelict in his duties towards them, came sometimes between him and his new peace; and he even hesitated to avow to them his position, lest they should reproach him with the fact of his not having set before them the way to life eternal. At last he determined to avow his Saviour before his family.

Laura's birth-day came with the opening of spring; and it had been her great desire to make her first appearance down stairs on that day. Her wish was gratified. The

day dawned clear and bright and beautiful;
one of those early days which give such
promise of the summer glory.   Each one of
the famiiy vied with the other in transferring
the sunshine from without to within.   And
when Mr. Chauncey and Fred carried their
precious invalid down to the library, the
truest contentment was visible on every
face.   A bright fire was glowing in the
grate, lest Laura should feel the change
from her own warm room.   The most lux-
urious of arm-chairs was in the cosiest
corner, and fragrant flowers perfumed the
air.   The dining-room adjoined the library;
and although Laura was still too weak to
sit at the table, from her fireside nook she
watched the family to her heart's content.
After the early tea, arranged for the benefit of the sick one, they all clustered around
her, and pleasant, though rather quiet chat
was interchanged.   In a little while, Mr.

Chauncey drew near to Laura, placing himself between her and his wife; and taking the hand of each, he said:

"I have something to say to you all, dear ones. Will you listen to me?"

A hush fell upon them, for his voice was low.

"We have lived many years, as happy a household as could anywhere be found. We have been blessed in every respect. And yet we have given but little thought to the Giver of our blessings. Not until we had nearly lost one of our number did I realize what I was about; that I was living only for happiness in this world, and that it was fleeting. But now I have sought and found the real source of happiness in Jesus Christ, who has forgiven all my sins. If I could command you all to do the same, how joyfully would I do it, so sure am I

21

that here only is real happiness to be found. But that I cannot do. I can only begin now to set you the example I should have set years ago. I can only say, ' As for me, I will serve the Lord.' May God lead my household to choose the same portion. I thank Him that one of my children has even started in advance of me. Henceforth, we will at least have a family altar. Let us pray.''

His own voice was choked, and his words were very few : Thanksgiving for Laura's presence with them once more, and an earnest petition that God would dwell among them, and sobs interrupted his words. As they rose from their knees, Kitty flung herself into her father's arms. The others sat as if awe-stricken. And Margaret, feeling that the immediate family should be alone at such an hour, and her heart almost bursting with thankfulness, stole away to her own room to commence a letter which should carry the most welcome tidings to her mother.

CHAPTER XIX.

—

"My darling Margery:

Father and Mother are writing to Uncle Henry this morning, and I must tell you, dear, how thankful your letter made us. Truly, God is good to those who put their trust in Him. It was so sad to me to think of Uncle Henry not being a Christian. I have prayed for him a great deal since we were in New York. And I did believe he would, some day, be all we longed to see him. And yet, I think I must have prayed very faithlessly; for I was surprised when the news came. How queer it is that we profess to believe God when He promises to answer our prayers, and yet we almost always are astonished when the answer comes. I wasn't half so much so about Kitty. I somehow expected that. But we are all so thankful. Did you know that Uncle Henry had himself written to Mother? But recitation-bell is ringing, and anyhow, I guess Mother wants to tell you herself what he said. So good-bye, precious.

Your own WALTER."

"Yes, my precious child, I do want to tell you what your uncle says. And my heart is full, and my eyes overflowing, as I write. He says:

'Next to God, my dear sister, I believe I owe what I now am, most of all, to your child. Her unflinching consistency first made me believe that all true Christianity

was not yet dead; that religion was not to
be set aside as an old fashion, or a worn-out
garment. I had seen so much falseness that
I had said (in my haste) "All men are
liars." But her life helped me to believe
in the source of all truth. It paved my
way, more than anything else did, to the
foot of the cross. I could instance little
things to you which she never dreamed that
I noticed; but it is not necessary. She is
a precious child, dear Helen. God long
preserve her to you.'

Darling Margery, this is enough to make
you thank God every day of your life.
Give my very warmest love to all; and to
dear Kitty a tender greeting.

MOTHER."

" Margery dear, I am just as glad as the
rest. But O, Madge, I want you so. Isn't
your visit almost over? I do believe this

bright warm weather will bring the May flowers out, and you must be here to gather them. Isn't the city hot and horrid now? And don't you and Kitty both need country air? For I want Kitty here. I want to take her on some of our famous rides. Isn't somebody coming home with you? Dear me! I don't see why people who love each other have to live so far apart. Do come home, Madge. Uncle Henry has had you long enough, I'm sure. And I am just tired of doing without you.

Rob."

"My own dear child:

God has given you grace to let your light shine, and that fills me with as much joy as the news about your uncle and Kitty.

Our spring is early this year, and it reminds us that we only gave you up for the winter. I think you wrote us that your various quarters in your lessons would soon come to an end. I do not want to hurry you home if you are not ready, nor do any of us; and there is no need of haste. But we shall not be sorry to see you. And now I have a plan to propose which I think equal in brilliancy to your uncle's raid upon you last fall. Why should he not come, with all the family, and make Rowenah their summer quarters? A quiet summer will probably do Laura more good than a succession of jaunts; and we should all enjoy being together, I am sure. I wish our house was big enough to hold them all. But we can hardly make them comfortable; certainly not as comfortable as they can be at the hotel. They will not do much more than eat and sleep there, of course; we shall claim most of their time. Suggest the idea to Uncle Henry and Aunt Alice, and let us know their views of it. If you should want to come home soon I think I can promise to run down for you within the next three weeks. Aunt Dinah is beginning to think you are never coming. You will not find her looking any older than when you went away; at least I cannot see any change. Good-night, my child. I dare not say what a difference it will make to us all to have you with us.

Your FATHER.

Such were the contents of what Fred called Margaret's home budget, within a few days after Laura's birth-day. The same thoughts with regard to the time having come for her visit to expire had been running in her mind, and she had only been waiting for Laura to be a little more fully restored before suggesting the idea. The winter had been a very happy one, and she could not leave her uncle's house without much regret; but her heart turned longingly homeward. And her cousins felt that they could not, without great selfishness, urge her to linger. Kitty only made one stipulation, to which Margaret was more than willing to accede.

"You will not go till after Communion Sabbath, dear, please. I must have you here then."

Accordingly she wrote to her father that if he could arrange his plans to join them about that time, she would be ready to return with him in the course of the following week. To her intense delight, he wrote that the arrangement would suit him perfectly; and that if Uncle Henry and Aunt Alice would accept a visit now, instead of the one declined at Christmas, he and Mrs. Worthington would both come for Margaret.

A happy meeting it was. A happy day

when so many of them assembled at Christ's table. Kitty was baptized. She and her father were received into the church: and Margaret could not but think of the contrast between her first communion in that church, and this, her last. Then she had sat in loneliness in the pew. Now the presence of two seemed to be a pledge that all her uncle's family should be gathered into the visible church of Christ on earth, and finally, into the assembly of the redeemed in Heaven.

All but Laura were in church. She was scarcely able for the long service; and she was not sorry to have an excuse for staying away. Her conscience smote her very often. But she steeled herself against it, and determined not to let her mind dwell upon these matters. If she could have forgotten Margaret's devotion to her during her illness, she would have felt vexed with her.

But that was impossible. So she merely withdrew more and more into herself, and determinately avoided all possibilities of quiet talks with Margaret, or indeed with Kitty, lest the dreaded subject should be introduced.

When the communicants left the church Fred was once more at Margaret's side.

"Will you let me have my last walk home with you?" he said.

"Indeed I will, Fred, this is such a lovely day."

"It is so," he said. "Spring is really here."

She could not, at first, talk much. It seemed to her as if it would be sacrilege to let words on ordinary topics cross her lips; and how to speak of other matters she scarcely knew. But it might be her last opportunity, and she dared not neglect it.

"Do you remember the first Communion

Sunday, when you came to meet me here, Fred?"

" Of course I do, Margery. Why?"

" I was thinking of the contrast between that and this, and how happy it made me ; and then, how far from satisfied I feel yet."

"About what?"

He knew very well, but he was willing to hear her say it.

" O, Fred, I cannot be happy till I see you all where Uncle Henry and Kitty are to-day."

" I believe you, Mag. And just once in a while I think I won't be happy myself till I am there. I don't make any promises. But I'll tell you one thing. If I ever do get there you will have had a big hand in it. You and Walter. Walter's letter about Sam Evans was too good for a sinner like me even to read. I don't know why you showed it to me. But part of it struck, —

don't you know what he said about praying for Sam? I kind of imagined then that you and he had a way of praying for some other fellows. And then, when Walter was here he gave me a sort of lecture. And, well, I shouldn't wonder if I thought about such thing sometimes."

"Fred, all I am afraid is that 'some time' will suffice for you. I want you to think of them now."

"Well, suppose I want to. How can I make myself do it."

"Just as you can 'make yourself' take any step in that direction, Fred. Ask, and it shall be given you."

"You believe that, do you?"

"Believe what?"

"That things that you ask for are given?"

"O, Fred! how could I help believing it? Don't I know it from my own experience

every day of my life?   Think of the great
blessings of to-day; and I could tell you of
others, innumerable.   Only try it for yourself, Fred; that's all I ask.   You will soon
know how true it is.   And as to what you
said about Walter and myself praying for
other people, Fred, if it ever helps you to
remember that we are praying for you, you
need never doubt it."

"Well, Margery," he said, "I don't
really know what I am, or how much I
care for these things.   Like as not something in business or in society will put them
all out of my heart to-morrow.   But I know
I ought to think about them.   You had
better give me a reminder now and then.
It won't do any harm; and though I said I
wouldn't make any promises, I will promise
now not to let any of them make me mad,
as your first reminders did."

"What do you mean, Fred? I never spoke to you about these things before."

"That's true. But you know there is a saying that 'Actions speak louder than words.' I won't specify anything; but if anybody does ever make me less of a sinner than I am, I guess I know who that somebody will be."

On Tuesday Mr. and Mrs. Worthington and Margaret were to leave New York; and on Monday Dr. Harris dined, by invitation, at Mr. Chauncey's. Sam Evans was also there. In the course of the evening Mr. Worthington took occasion to say to Dr. Harris:

"I am very much struck with the change for the better in young Evans. You know we had trouble with him in college, and I feared the effect of the temptations of the city upon him. But his whole bearing now is that of a man, and a man who means to be something, too."

"I believe he has taken a step upwards," was the answer. "His employers like him very much, and his habits seem to be excellent. He is much favored in his employers. They are Christian men, who look upon their clerks, not merely as hirelings, but as immortal beings, for whose souls they are, in no small degree, responsible. Evans attends my church regularly, and is an earnest listener. And from a conversation I had with him a short time ago, I have great hopes that he is not without serious thought. I think he is a young man who is very easily influenced for good or evil; who needs every possible help upwards. One of our librarians from the Mission School is going abroad for a year, very soon, and I have urged the superintendent to propose Evans as a successor. He may, in this way, become inter-

ested in our mission; and may get, as well
as do, good."

"I think that is an excellent idea. And
I do hope he will continue to do well. I
knew his father, formerly; and am, therefore, much interested in Sam."

" Your son is his great helper, I think.
He cannot say enough in his praise; and he
is anxious to deserve his good opinion.
' Walter stood by me when scarcely any
one else did,' he said to me the other night.
' And I never do a wrong thing now without feeling that it is treating him badly. He
lets me be his friend, and I don't want him
to be ashamed of me.' If Christian young
men would only realize their opportunities
for doing good, Mr. Worrthington, — "

They were interrupted by demands made
upon them by some of the others, and soon
the evening was a thing of the past.

The parting came on Tuesday. It was

altogether sorrowful to the Chaunceys, but Margaret's heart was throbbing with a tumult of mixed emotions. She dared not anticipate her arrival at Rowenah, and the meeting with the dear ones there. And yet it was harder than ever to leave her uncle's family. Scenes of parting are better imagined than described. So we will not repeat the farewells, but will only add that there was a fair promise of Mr. Worthington's plan of a re-union at Rowenah in the summer, whither, who knows but you and I may some day follow them?